The Boy in the Suitcase

To Memie Lee —
Who fights the best
battles! Thank you!
March 24, 2018

N. V. Baker

THE CONCEALING SEA, BOOK 1

Nightwatchman Press
NEW MEXICO

Book cover design: Joanna Pasek (www.akwarelki.net)
Book Layout: BookDesignTemplates.com

The Boy in the Suitcase/ N. V. Baker. -- 1st ed.
ISBN 978-0-9979936-2-2

To Betty Sue, for her kindness & wisdom, and being there for me since the beginning

*And the beauty and mystery of the ships, and the
magic of the sea.*

—HENRY WADSWORTH LONGFELLOW
My Lost Youth

GULF OF FINLAND
From *The Essential Atlas of the World* (Barnes & Noble 2005)

1

Staring into the dark pewter waters of the Baltic Sea, Magdalena Albright leaned against the varnished wood railing and contemplated how much drowning would hurt.

It was an academic question. There was a time when it wasn't, and she still bore a faint scar on her left wrist to prove it. But now, in the soft early daylight of late spring in the far north, she had no intention of jumping.

Still, the question fascinated her: how would drowning feel?

Lena stood high above the waterline, on the fifteenth deck of a megaship. Here, plexiglass walls along the railing kept guests safe and somewhat shielded from buffeting winds. But there were periodic breaks in the transparent wall to let in breezes; through one of them, she could peer down at the sea.

She considered the impact of a body's collision with water from this height. Probably like hitting concrete: bones would break, internal organs burst. Then would come body- wrenching iciness, salty strangulation, pulmonary spasms, heart seizure.

That is, if one would even hit the water from here. She scanned the length of the massive ship, noting its dense belt of life boats, white bellied and red topped, like giant vitamin capsules. In all likelihood, a jumper would miss the sea entirely, instead smashing into one of them. It would be ironic, she thought, to be killed by a life boat.

"You aren't going to jump, are you?"

Lena jerked, startled. She had thought she was alone. After all, it was not even six in the morning. The ship wouldn't arrive in St. Petersburg for another hour.

Swiveling her head, she saw him, a blond boy, dressed in a green polo shirt, tan windbreaker, jeans, and black and yellow trainers. It was the cute kid she had met the day before yesterday in the medieval Rakvere castle on the Estonian shore excursion. His parents had loitered in the castle yard smoking with another woman while the boy explored. Lena found herself next to him in the torture chamber, examining a rack of spikes designed to elicit confessions from heretics. They'd been among the few in their group to venture further into the castle's Hell Maze with its creepy sound effects, uneven floor and manikin body parts dangling from the ceiling. In the darkness, they had bumped into each other and laughed, and they now shared a secret history of having survived hell.

Lena nodded in greeting and took his question seriously. "Nope. Just looking."

"Oh. That's good then." The kid came next to her and stood on tiptoes to peer down, too. "I saw someone once who jumped, from a building, not a boat."

"Oh, God, I'm sorry," she said reflexively.

"It wasn't someone I knew. Just a guy on the internet." He chewed on his lip. "It sucked."

"The person dying? Or dying that way?"

"Both. Look," he said, changing the topic. "Do you think I could go with you to St. Petersburg today? Like at the castle?"

Lena was a little taken aback at the request. "Aren't your folks going?"

"They thought the castle was boring. They thought there'd be crown jewels and stuff. So today they're hanging around the ship."

Lena was puzzled. "Today's shore excursion goes to Catherine Palace, and it's supposed to be stunning. Tell them that. I bet they'll change their minds." She hoped they would. The kid was all right, but she was hoping to encounter the man she'd met the day before at the wine-tasting luncheon. Marcus was his name.

The boy didn't move. "Nah, that's okay," he shrugged, then stuck out a slender hand. "I'm Carter Massek."

The formality of the gesture made her smile. She took his small hand and they shook. "Nice to meet you, Carter Massek. I'm Lena Albright."

"Lena Albright." He seemed to be memorizing the name. "Why do you dress like that?"

Glancing down at her black boots, long black skirt, black lace gloves and black leather jacket, she knew why he had asked. No one else on board looked like her. "I like to, that's why. And why do you dress like that?" She gestured at his windbreaker and polo shirt, then gently teased, "You look like a dad."

"Well, you look like a vampire," he retorted.

"You've discovered my secret!" she shouted dramatically and made a playful lunge for his throat. He yelped in surprise and then laughed.

She tucked her hair behind her ears. "Actually, I'm goth. Do you know what that means?"

He paused for a moment. "A Satanist? My mom said that when she saw you at the castle. I think she was joking but I can't always tell."

Zipping her jacket against a cold gust, Lena considered how best to answer. "Being goth is sort of the opposite. We're a community. We share music and certain values and aesthetics. We don't hurt anyone."

"I think you're cool."

"Thanks, Carter. I think you're cool, too." Then, checking her purple phone for the time, she added, "I've got to go back to my room for a bit."

"So, I can go with you? To St. Petersburg, I mean?" He sounded anxious.

"If it's okay with your folks." Why not, she thought. After all, what was the chance of seeing Marcus on this tour, out of a dozen cruise-sponsored tours of St. Petersburg? "We can meet for breakfast about six-thirty in the Galley Buffet. But you'll need your passport and other documents to show your parents' approval."

"Sure!" the boy said with enthusiasm. "Thanks!"

Lena turned to go back inside, then shouted back to him. "I'll be sitting on the left."

"Port side! Okay!"

Strange kid, Lena thought to herself as she took the stairs to her stateroom three floors down. Most boys wouldn't want to hang out with a woman who was thirty years older. He must be lonely. She laughed ruefully at herself as she swiped her key card. "And most adults wouldn't want to hang out with a kid." Maybe she was lonely, too.

Throwing her jacket on the bed, Lena pulled a bulky black sweater over her head. The air was cooler than she'd expected and the jacket alone wasn't that warm. She gave herself a quick assessment in the room's large mirror, brushed a hand through her long black hair, checked her eye makeup and put on blue lipstick, her favorite. She had other colors. Red, of course, also purple. She didn't wear much black lipstick anymore, but she had it with her, in case.

Then she fell back on the king-sized bed. She had to admit it to herself. She was lonely. She hadn't felt this isolated since high school. Everyone on this cruise was so damn perky. And judgmental. Satanist, indeed. Why had she come on a cruise anyway?

Lena knew the answer to that. The plan had been to bring her niece along, as a college graduation gift. She was resolved to reach out more to family. It had started with the Christmas eve breakup with Dave. About the same time, two of her closest friends had gotten married and moved to Canada. Many of the others in the community had long since discarded their goth identities and now worked at banks, law offices, medical supply houses. There still was a vibrant community in the Los Angeles area, but, at thirty-nine years old, she was the elder, the one who mentored the next generation. And that work was increasingly on-line, through her goth music blog.

No wonder she felt isolated.

Lena wasn't close to her family, emotionally or geographically. But she was working on that. Especially with her older sister and niece, who both lived in Miami. So, when her niece had expressed interest in a Baltic cruise, Lena had leapt at it, making all the arrangements to fly from L.A. and take her.

The problem was, her niece had changed. When she was young, she used to love visiting Lena, but years of prep school and a private East Coast college had made her more conservative in her tastes. Spending eight days at sea with her eccentric aunt no longer appealed to her, and she - politely - declined the gift. The rebuff stung. For a while, Lena's sister

Pauline had planned to take her place. A sister cruise, Pauline had called it. But then an important case had come up and Pauline, a high-powered attorney, had had to bail out as well. To her credit, she had felt awful about it and paid for the stateroom, with its balcony and king-sized bed.

Lena wanted to cancel the whole thing but Pauline insisted she at least try to have a good time. Visiting this part of the world. Meeting a nice man.

Lena conceded that she was enjoying the shore excursions, more than she had expected. And Pauline's comment about meeting a nice man struck home. Dave hadn't been good company the last few years. And before Dave were Randy and Samson, both self-centered disasters as boyfriends. Initial signs on the ship had been promising; there were other singles on board. Before long, though, Lena doubted anything romantic would happen. In fact, other passengers seemed to avoid her. Maybe they thought she was a Satanist, too.

Yesterday, that changed. As they cruised east toward Russia, the ship offered multiple entertainments to occupy passengers in lieu of shore excursions. On a whim, she'd signed up for the wine-tasting luncheon. Seated next to her was Marcus, a good-looking man with salt and pepper hair. He was thoughtful and serious, not irritatingly chipper like others she'd met on board, probably because he was traveling with his elderly father. From oblique references, Lena gathered that his father – who had not attended the luncheon – was in the early stages of dementia. Marcus had casually explained that he had chosen an ocean view room with no balcony. Lena surmised it was because he was afraid his father might fall overboard. That conversation probably triggered her musings this morning.

She'd searched for Marcus last night, strolling through the Charthouse main dining hall and past the ship's other restaurants and bars. She'd finally settled at the centrally located Atrium Bar, thinking he might walk by. But all she generated was some awkward flirtation from a guy who was built like a boulder. And even he left after his girlfriend or wife signaled to him from across the room.

So much for Marcus. She didn't even know his last name. It was unlikely she'd ever see him again, among the almost four thousand passengers on board.

The ship's public-address system screeched to life with a cheery male voice:

Good morning, Sea Dream Cruisers! The Sea Dream has arrived at port in St. Petersburg, Russia. All of those planning to take the fantastic shore excursions into St. Petersburg are reminded to check their tickets for their muster points. Don't forget to bring your passports. Passengers may begin disembarkation at seven

THE BOY IN THE SUITCASE | 13

on deck four. Please keep the stairways clear!
Remember to be back on board by five o'clock.
Happy sailing!

St. Petersburg. This was what Lena was waiting
for, the highlight for her of the cruise. The tragedy of
the last Romanovs had always touched her. She
glanced at her phone; it was almost time to meet the
kid.

2

The Galley Buffet on deck fifteen aft was packed, and Lena had difficulty negotiating her tray through the swarms of fellow diners and their own precariously balanced plates. Finally, spying the wave of a smallish hand, she made her way to a table by an outsized window looking onto the St. Petersburg quay, rows of apartment skyscrapers in the distance.

"Hello, again," she said to Carter as she sat. For some reason, she hadn't noticed before how downright beautiful the boy was. Thick dark lashes, light hazel eyes and smooth skin. His pale gold hair was trimmed short, but Lena could see the hint of curl if it grew longer. His face was perfectly proportioned. It simply wasn't fair, she thought; no boy should be prettier than any girl she had ever met.

After motioning to a staff member circulating the room with a coffee pot, she asked Carter where his parents were.

"Sleeping in. They stay up late. They like to gamble." He took a bite of blueberry pancake. "It's okay, though. They signed all the paperwork so I can go today." On the table next to his orange juice, beneath his tan camouflage mobile phone, were a few folded sheets of paper and his American passport.

His parents' disengagement seemed peculiar to her. Wouldn't normal parents have wanted to meet her before entrusting their son to her care? Wondering if this was a sign of child neglect, she ventured a question. "So, how old are you anyway?"

With a hint of aggression in his voice, Carter replied, "How old do you think I am?"

She didn't dare underestimate his age. Kids were sensitive about being seen as younger than they were. To flatter him, she made an exaggerated guess. "About twelve?" In reality, he seemed closer to nine.

He looked shocked. "How did you know?"

She was equally shocked but better at hiding it. She shrugged and tried to make her voice casual. "So, you're twelve." Not too young, she thought; the news relieved her main concern about the parents.

"I will be tomorrow. This is my birthday cruise. We go on one every year, since I turned seven."

"Well, happy birthday early. You must like cruising."

He shook his head. "Not really. But my parents do. And they leave me alone, let me do what I want on a cruise. I like that part."

Another slightly odd answer, Lena thought. "Well, it's my first cruise," she confessed.

"Yeah, I guessed," he said, slurping orange juice.

"It's that obvious?"

"You're not like anyone else," he explained, and then said, "The creepy woman is following me."

Momentarily flustered by his swerve off-topic, Lena paused before asking, "Do you mean the woman you pointed out at the castle? The one who's friends with your parents?" He hadn't called her creepy then; Lena wondered what had happened.

"She's not my parents' friend. She just met them a few days ago. Now, when she sees my mom, she's like, *oh, darling!*" he added in a high fake voice.

"But isn't that how things are on a cruise? People meet, become friendly, then they go their separate ways and never see each other again. It's no big deal."

"Then why does she keep asking *me* to go into St. Petersburg with her? Why doesn't she ask my *parents*?"

"I don't know. Maybe she knows they don't want to go but you do. Maybe she likes you."

He twisted his mouth in a funny expression. "Nobody likes me."

"I like you." Lena was telling the truth. There was something feral about his manner - bold but wary, even skittish - that appealed to her. For a kid, that is; she usually didn't hang around kids.

"You're different, like I said. You're not all sweet and phony. You don't talk down to me. And you don't pry into my private life."

Pry into his private life? Good God, he was only eleven. Lena let it pass. "Maybe she knows St. Petersburg. Is she Russian?"

Carter shook his head. "She sounds American but I don't know. Maybe it's an act, like being my parents' friend."

Lena was intrigued. "Why don't you like her?"

"I just don't." He stopped and scooted down in his seat. "Don't turn around! She's here!"

Lena had to fight the immediate urge to swivel her head. She was curious about this woman, and why she upset Carter so much.

He hissed. "I told you. I told you she's stalking me!"

Lena ignored his agitated whispers and took the smart phone from her bag, turned on the selfie setting and used that to study the woman seated at the table behind her. The image surprised her. She guessed she was expecting an old witch or cold-eyed killer. Instead, the woman looked youngish, probably mid-thirties. With her slight overbite, she was cute rather than beautiful. She had a rosy complexion and curly dark auburn hair in a stylish cut. A little plump, even voluptuous, like the subject of a painting by Peter Paul Rubens.

Glasses perched on her nose, the woman was preoccupied tapping a message into her own phone, looking up only when a balding older man approached her table carrying a coffee cup. He must have asked her if he could sit because she motioned toward a vacant chair. In that brief interim between his question and her answer, the woman looked straight at Lena. Then she turned to watch as the man set his coffee down.

There was something about the woman, about her direct appraisal of her, that unsettled Lena a little. Had she seen this woman before? Then Lena scolded herself for succumbing to Carter's paranoia.

"You're over-reacting," she reassured the boy as she put away her phone. "The woman seems ordinary enough, a solo traveler like me, just making friends."

Carter didn't respond. He stayed low in his seat, peering over the table top past their empty dishes.

Lena finished her coffee and folded her napkin. "Ready to go?" she asked as she prepared to push back her chair. Before Carter could reply, the cute plump woman was next to her, looking down at Carter with a friendly open expression.

"Why, good morning," the woman said cheerfully. "I didn't see you there at first. Aren't we going into St. Petersburg today? There's so many fabulous things to see."

"I'm going with her," Carter replied, indicating Lena with his chin.

A brief pause. "I see," the woman said. "Is this a new friend?" She turned toward Lena and put out her hand. "My name's Kellie Rose Roberts, from Oklahoma City. Well, originally from Boston, by way of

Chicago, but that's a long story. I'm a friend of Jay and Janelle's."

Keeping her eyes on Kellie Rose Roberts, Lena heard Carter mutter, "My parents."

The woman seemed pleasant enough to Lena, although a little chatty and her handshake felt limp. She introduced herself, "It's nice to meet you, Kellie. I'm Lena Albright."

"Kellie Rose," the woman softly corrected. "And I'm absolutely delighted to meet you, Lena."

"Would you like to join me and Carter?" Lena gestured at an empty seat, ignoring Carter's angry head shakes. Secretly, she regretted making the offer as well and hoped the woman would decline. She didn't want them to be late for their tour group.

The woman's smile widened. "Gosh, no. But thanks," Kellie Rose said, turning toward her table and the man with the coffee. "You two have fun," she called over her shoulder. "We'll catch up later. Bye, Lena. Bye for now, Carter."

Carter was sullen as they left the Galley Buffet for their muster point in the Charthouse eight decks below. When they got in the elevator, he lashed out. "Why did you do that? Why did you invite her to sit down? Why did you tell her my name?"

The accusation shocked Lena. "Your name? If she knows your parents, she already knows your name."

"Carter is my private name. Only my friends can call me that."

"I'm sorry. I didn't know. So, what's your real name?"

"Carter is my real name."

"Okay then, the name your parents call you?"

"I hate it." He said nothing else.

What a secretive kid, she thought. She let the name thing pass. "Well, Carter, I have to tell you I think your fear of the woman is...," she almost said ridiculous, but caught herself, "unfounded. Kellie Rose seems perfectly nice."

"Like a cobra," the child mumbled as the elevator doors opened on deck seven.

"I'll keep that in mind," Lena assured him, then pointed toward the Charthouse dining hall, where people were already gathering amid polished tables and nautical maps. "Look. We're in time for Group A."

They hurried their steps toward the gathering crowd.

3

"God damn coffin," Eddie Alphonso Boltman
griped as he slumped on the edge of the mattress. Except under the bed where he'd stashed his
large suitcase, space in the windowless studio on deck
five was tight, filled by his massive frame. He had to
go to the ship's fucking gym just to stretch. She had
a stateroom, he thought resentfully. "Why the fuck
can't I have a stateroom?" Eddie had lately taken to
muttering to himself. He missed not having a partner
to talk to. A real partner, not the Bitch.

And she was a bitch, too, Aurora Borealis. He
suspected that wasn't even her real name. Another
gripe, because she knew his real name. But, anyway,
it didn't matter. In his head, she was the Bitch, always giving him orders. She thought she was so much
smarter than he was. Well, he'd show her. He wasn't
new at this game. He'd done it maybe half a dozen
times before. And just because he'd screwed up one
fucking time, they saddled him with her. He should
call Management to complain. He had their phone
number somewhere. If they hadn't changed it already. They did that sometimes.

Last night he almost lost it. There he was in the
Atrium Bar, bored out of his skull, when a tall pale

woman comes in. Not much meat on her bones, but she looked like the type who wouldn't mind a good fuck: alone, not too old, and dressed all in black. Fire engine red lips, oh boy. Long black hair, too, probably dyed, he didn't care. She'd smiled – well, a little, anyway – when he asked if the seat next to her was taken. He was just starting to make nice with her when he sees the Bitch in the distance pointing at him like he's a fucking dog. Okay, so he followed her out. But he should have ignored her, pretended that he didn't notice. Just let her stew.

"You know the rules," she'd hissed once they were alone. "No sex. No drinking. You have a job to do."

"I'm fucking dying here," he'd told her. "I gotta do something or I'm going to explode."

"The only thing you *got* to do is obey orders. You got that?"

"Fuck it," he'd said. "I'll quit. I'll get off at the next port. Then where will you be?"

She'd given him a hard look. "Go ahead. Leave the ship. Just don't count on ever working with us again."

Eddie had come close to smacking her. This morning, surveying his hefty fist, he muttered, "She's fucking lucky I didn't." He was lucky, too, he realized, because he needed this job. He had bills to pay and the money was so freaking good.

4

Over and over in her head ran a favorite song lyric: *Mother Russia, Mother Russia, Mother Russia rain down down down.*

It was from the Sisters of Mercy. Lena was in high school when she'd first heard them; really embraced their attitude and ethic when she went to college and met other outsiders. It was so liberating to finally admit - no, more than that - to *embrace* the strangeness she had always felt inside, instead of always pretending to be normal, whatever that was. She finally felt she belonged.

But she knew she didn't belong here in Catherine Palace. With the rest of an enormous herd, Lena shuffled in brown paper booties over the intricate parquet floor of the Great Hall, the famous Hall of Light. Its walls were intricate as well, adorned floor to ceiling with gold leaf garlands and filigreed mirrors. Overhead were time-darkened frescoes of imperial glory. This was the grandest of the palace's public spaces, intended to convey the majesty of the Romanovs to visiting lesser monarchs and Russian aristocrats.

Despite the grand scale of the palace, Lena felt suffocated. In the ornately ornamented interior, there was no room for the imagination, no room for the nonconformist, no room even for the soul of Mother Russia. Instead, Mother Russia had been consigned to the villages, possibly exiled to Siberia. She certainly wasn't here.

And that sorely disappointed Lena. She had imagined this visit differently. Not a hagiography of czars and czarinas, embodied in gilt and precious stones and carved amber. But a glimpse into the lives of the human beings who had lived and suffered here, epitomized in their ordinary artifacts. She found herself lingering over the few everyday items on display - a doll, an ink stand, a toy horse.

Her preference for modest mementos wasn't shared. Cameras and phones clicked around her, the crowds gawking at the gold and murmuring in awe and delight. She wondered what Marcus thought about the place. He'd mentioned in passing that his father's family had emigrated from Russia at the time of the First World War, and his father had long dreamed of seeing St. Petersburg. Lena's eyes swam over the various tour groups crowding into the Great Hall. Disappointed, she saw no sign of Marcus.

Her group was herded through other elegant rooms. Eventually, they trundled into a dining room where a white-clothed table in the center had been set for just two, poised for the arrival of a nonexistent royal couple. A more human-scale space, Lena thought. While almost the square footage as her Burbank apartment, the room was comparatively intimate for Catherine Palace, and the gold flourishes were kept to a minimum.

Suddenly, Lena remembered Carter. She should be looking out for him. He was so small, he easily could get separated from the others. Scanning the jostling crowd in the dining room, she finally caught sight of his blonde head and green shirt. He was frowning at the imaginary people at the table.

"You okay?" she asked, walking over.

With a serious expression, he looked up and shrugged. "I'm okay."

He was an outsider like her, she suddenly realized, deeply uncomfortable about something. She sensed what it might be, but she didn't pry and didn't presume. That wasn't part of the ethic she followed. He'd tell her or not in his own time.

But she was curious about his take on the palace. "What do you think?" she asked, gesturing at the dining room's pistachio green walls and pink accents and, beyond the grand doorway, the full expanse of the fairytale palace. "Like it?"

He seemed startled to be asked. "No, I ..." he abruptly stopped, self-conscious.

Lena noticed his reticence, his reluctance to disagree. To encourage him, she confessed, "I'm not crazy about the place either."

Carter nodded, then critically regarded the luxury. "Didn't our guide say it cost, like, millions of rubles to build?" he asked. "And they put a hundred kilos of gold on the stucco outside? The stucco?!"

Lena sensed where he was going. "That's true. Catherine Palace is extravagant."

"Not just here, though. There are dozens of palaces around St. Petersburg, right?"

"Right," she said. The Romanovs wasted a lot of money on palaces. Even so, she felt she had to defend the vision of Peter the Great. "Regardless, this is a great city and a UNESCO World Heritage Site, with one of the most famous art museums in the world."

"It was built by serfs and prisoners of war," Carter bluntly countered.

Lena knew a little imperial history, too. "Okay, but don't forget that Peter the Great did some good things. He constructed the seaport. Banned arranged marriages. Passed land reforms so women could inherit. And…"

He broke in, impatient. "But what about the serfs? He didn't free them. And later, when they were free, they were forced to work in terrible factories."

She gravely nodded. "Then you know there was a revolution in 1917. When the Romanovs were brutally executed?"

"Sure. I mean, I'm sorry they were killed and all, the czar and his family. But they kind of brought it on themselves. Don't you think so?"

His comments shocked her. "You can't mean that," Lena chided. "The youngest child, Alexei, was only thirteen." Not much older than you are, she considered adding.

He sighed, fidgeted, nodded. "All right. Not him. But at the coronation party for Nicolas, over a thousand people were trampled to death. Did you know that? And what about Bloody Sunday, when people were just trying to give him a petition and his guards shot them dead?"

"Where do you get this?" Lena knew some Russian history, but she hadn't read this.

"I like history. I watch documentaries."

Lena looked again at the gold-rimmed china service and silver implements. Could she be wrong, and the Bolsheviks were justified in murdering the Romanovs? She had always felt drawn to their tragedy. Just this morning, at the Saint Peter and Paul Fortress, she'd been deeply moved by the white caskets with their ponderous gold crosses. She had spent minutes examining the nearby photographs of the five children, looking for any sign that they sensed the impending tragedy.

But now Lena wondered if she had been romanticizing the Romanovs too much. Carter's observations had unsettled her a little, exposed her to another side of the story. She wasn't ready to agree with him that they brought the disaster on themselves. After all, Nicolas had abdicated and was in Siberia with his family when the executioners came. But Carter's point reminded her that she shouldn't take stories at face value. She should investigate for herself.

"Well," she sighed. "I think it's tough to know what's right. They were victims of their times, murdered for the sins of their parents and grandparents and so on. And who can control the actions of their parents?"

Carter thought for a moment. "You can't. But you don't have to become like your parents. Know what I mean?"

With a pensive smile, Lena answered. "Yes, in fact, I do." She certainly had followed a different path than her family. She gave him a long look, "You're a smart kid, you know that?"

Their guide's voice broke in; their group was on the move.

"Thanks," Carter said simply and then - unexpectedly - took her hand and led the way through a high crested doorway into another Rococo wonderland.

5

"I'm tired. I want to go to bed now," Pavel Vanin complained. He looked plaintively at his son as he absently scratched a dry patch of skin on his wrist.

Marcus took his father's hand for a moment to stop the incessant scratching. He heard the exhaustion in his voice and wasn't surprised. It had been a long day, starting with a three-hour tour of the Catherine Palace, then a quick lunch of vegetable borsch in a cavernous dining hall named for Pushkin, and ending with a two-hour hustle through the highlights of the Hermitage Museum. Rembrandt, da Vinci, Rafael and others whose names he couldn't recall; hurried steps past Egyptian antiquities, ancient Roman coins, suits of armor, Italian sculptures. Everything blurred together in his mind. He felt beat; no wonder his father did.

He looked at his father sympathetically. "I know, Pop. Soon, I promise. First, we need to get back on the ship."

The line to re-board was long and slow. Each person's key card had to be scanned, each bag and purse sent through an x-ray. His father listlessly shambled forward, Marcus at his elbow, both enveloped in the ennui of other returning passengers.

Marcus noticed his father fumbling in a jacket pocket, then pulling out a colorful wooden object the size and shape of an egg.

"What have you got there?" he asked curiously.

His father frowned. "I don't know."

Marcus took the piece. He recognized it: a carved Father Frost holiday ornament from the large display outside the souvenir shop on the wharf.

"Did you buy this?"

"I don't know," his father repeated. "It must have fallen into my pocket."

Marcus groaned. His father had shop-lifted it. He had the money in his wallet, but lately he had started to take things without paying. Marcus suspected it was easier for his father than figuring out unfamiliar currency.

"Why didn't you tell me you wanted it? I would have bought it for you. Now I have to take it back." He hated the idea of leaving the line to return to the shop, knowing that his father would follow and they both would lose their places. His father wouldn't get his nap anytime soon.

"Hi," came a voice. "It's Marcus, right?"

He turned around. Four people behind him stood the woman from the wine tasting, Lena. "Hey, there," he answered. A nice woman, he remembered, and interesting. He regretted missing the chance of talking more with her. "I can't stay to talk. My father picked this up without paying, so I've got to go."

Lena glanced back at the duty-free shop, and again at Marcus and his obviously fading father. "Stay there. I have an idea," she said. She took the Father Frost and, turning to the boy standing next to her, handed it to him with a wad of euros. She knew tourist places near the ship accepted various currencies. "Can you take this to the shop over there and say that your grandfather forgot to pay for it?"

The kid was gone in a flash.

Marcus felt a surge of gratitude. "Thanks a lot, Lena. My father really needs a nap so I didn't want to lose our place in line."

"No worries. He'll be back in a jiff." Lena was pleased he remembered her name.

Marcus tried to hand her a fifty-euro note. She waved her hand dismissively. "Let's wait to see what it actually cost. I'm sure it's not that much."

Good thing his father didn't pocket one of those expensive Faberge-style eggs, Marcus realized. "Is that your son?" he asked.

"No, he's a friend. We visited the city together today. Carter's parents stayed on the ship."

"Nice kid," Marcus added.

"Yes, he is," Lena said. "So, where did your group go today?"

"Catherine Palace and the Hermitage. You?"

"St. Peter and Paul Fortress and then Catherine Palace. Quite a whirlwind tour of both. What did you think?"

"They're pretty overwhelming, actually. My father was taken with all the grandeur. Well, honestly, so was I. Never seen anything quite like either place before."

"It's like living inside a Faberge egg," Lena said and Marcus nodded appreciatively. Then she added, "I think all that opulence upset Carter a little. The brutal exploitation of serfs and workers. He made a case for the Bolshevik Revolution."

"That kid did?" Marcus was impressed. "When I was his age, I would have been all about the suits of armor."

"I know. He's different."

At that moment, Marcus's father left the line and wandered over to Lena. "Do I know you, my dear? My name is Pavel. It's a pleasure to make your acquaintance."

"I'm Lena. And it's a pleasure to meet you too, Pavel."

With bright curiosity, he looked Lena up and down, appraising her outfit, her height. "My, my. You're what we used to call a tall drink of water."

Beneath her ivory makeup, Lena blushed. "Uh, thanks ...?"

Embarrassed for his father, Marcus quickly intervened. "Hey, Pop, come back."

His father ignored him. He clearly preferred chatting with Lena. "So, where are you going today?"

Lena stumbled a little, unsure what to say. "I'm just waiting in line to get back on the ship."

"This one? Well, that's amazing. How long have you been on the ship?"

"Since Copenhagen. The start of the cruise."

"What a coincidence! It's the same with me and my boy," and he waved vaguely toward Marcus. Then he whispered conspiratorially, "I'm on a secret mission to Russia, you know."

The woman behind Marcus sensed his anxiety and said. "It's fine. I'll save your spot." He nodded thanks and was next to his father in three quick steps.

"Pop...," he started to say.

Pavel had taken Lena's hand. "The KGB tortured me. But I didn't tell them a thing. I have to protect the president."

Before Lena could respond, Carter arrived breathless. He handed a small paper bag to the elderly man and the change to Lena.

Pavel promptly dropped Lena's hand, opened the bag and brought out the wooden ornament. "It's Santa Claus," he marveled, forgetting about the president and letting the paper bag fall to the tarmac.

Lena instinctively bent to pick it up and almost collided with Marcus. He was faster in reclaiming the litter and stuffed it into his pocket. Then he turned to Carter. "Thanks for helping us out. I owe you one, buddy." After pressing a twenty-euro bill into Lena's hand, he returned to his place in line. "Pop?" he said. "C'mon."

Pavel looked up from the Father Frost ornament and drifted toward Marcus just as the line moved forward. Marcus guided him by the elbow across the gangway and toward the security area. But before they disappeared into the ship, Marcus turned back to look at Lena. "Are you free this evening? Maybe we can get a drink. How about the Atrium Bar, about nine?"

Lena grinned. "The Atrium Bar at nine," she repeated.

6

Sidling up to Carter, Kellie Rose Roberts said softly, confidentially, "I hear you have a big birthday coming up." She was in the Masseks' stateroom, having pre-dinner cocktails with Janelle and Jay. And the kid. She sloshed the scotch in her glass, causing the ice cubes to tinkle.

Still in his windbreaker, as if he was simply passing through, Carter didn't glance up from the game on his phone. "Whatever," he shrugged.

"Twelve. That's a big deal. No longer a child." She took a delicate sip and ran her tongue over her upper lip.

Now he did stare at her. "I'm still a kid," he said more assertively than he felt. He wanted to still be a kid. He wasn't comfortable with what was happening to his body. Any day now, he might start bleeding. He dreaded that moment with all his might.

Kellie Rose studied his face. Discomfited, he looked back at his phone. She continued, "In some cultures, girls are married at that age."

The idea horrified Carter. "That's disgusting," he said.

"Of course, it is," she replied with a smooth smile. "Let's not talk about that. Did you know that

Stockholm has a museum of a famous sunken ship? It's called the Vasa. It's said to be quite extraordinary."

"Who cares?" Carter replied and turned away. He knew all about the Vasa, how it had been underwater for more than three hundred years, how it had been salvaged and restored. He had seen documentaries about the Vasa and was dying to see it. But he wouldn't tell her that; he didn't want her to take him.

Blinking slowly, Kellie Rose gave a small smile; she didn't look offended. "Oh, I think you do care," she said finally and then drifted over to Carter's father, Jay.

"So, what's this Vasa thing?" Jay asked quietly as he refreshed her drink.

"Don't be so rude, Jennifer," hissed Janelle in Carter's ear. "She's only being friendly."

He jerked back from his mother. "Don't call me that."

"Why do you say that? You're named for my best friend in college." When Carter didn't reply, she continued. "All I see when I look at you is my gorgeous girl. How is that so wrong?" She reached toward his forehead and stroked his short bangs. "I wish you'd grow your hair out longer. It's so beautiful; I wish I had hair like yours."

"Stop it!" Carter yanked away. His voice carried, and Jay was in front of him in a second.

"Don't you dare talk to your mother that way, young lady. She's gone out of her way to accommodate your demands on this trip. I don't know what else you expect us to do."

"Just leave me alone!" Carter dashed across the room and bunched into the far corner of the sofa, feet on the cushions, arms around his knees.

"What?! What have I done?" demanded Janelle, aggrieved.

Kellie Rose intervened. "Don't be too hard on her. She's a typical moody twelve-year-old on the cusp of womanhood. Hormones running wild. You remember that age."

Janelle gaped at Kellie Rose. "I don't remember that!" she said, pointing at Carter's feet and the black and yellow trainers. "Those are two sizes too big! Those are clown shoes!"

"Only half a size," Carter mumbled but no one heard.

"She has such dainty feet. And hands. She could be a top fashion model. She's that beautiful. And it's not just a mother's bias. Everyone says so."

Carter objected. "Lena doesn't." He was certain that Lena looked past all of that. She could see who he was inside.

Janelle fixed a steely gaze. "That woman is a bad influence on you, Jennifer, and I don't want you to see her again."

Jay was puzzled. "What woman? Whose Lena?"

"The one who looks like a devil worshipper. Didn't I say that from the start? How weird she is?" Janelle had thought Jennifer would go to St. Petersburg with Kellie Rose; that was the plan. But she had run off with that strange woman instead. Janelle's sense of grievance grew. "What is she doing hanging around our daughter all the time? Maybe she's in a cult."

"She's my friend! My only friend on this crappy boat!"

"Language, Jennifer," scolded Jay.

"I'm going with her tomorrow to Helsinki!"

Janelle was adamant. "No, you're not. You're going to celebrate your birthday with your family. Like a normal person. We'll go into Helsinki together. We'll go out to eat. We'll go shopping. I'll get you a new swim suit, maybe a bikini to show off your cute figure. You're outgrowing the old one. And don't make that face at me." Exhaling definitively, she turned to her friend. "Kellie Rose, would you like to come along?"

Before Kellie Rose could answer, Carter rushed to the stateroom's door. "I'm not going! You can't make me! I hate you all!" And he was gone.

7

On the fifteenth deck starboard, Lena watched the Russian shoreline recede as the ship sailed west, bound for Helsinki.

She wasn't thinking about the destination, though. Instead, she was mesmerized by the frothy white swirls forming on the water's jade surface. Too small to call white caps, they seemed to be an ancient script, perhaps a covert message to a celestial Viking. What if the Viking read it and returned? Now that would be interesting, she mused.

Despite her somber appearance, Lena loved to indulge in inventive play. In recent years, her work load – and Dave, with his snide remarks about her *acting her age* – had suppressed that penchant. But here, in the Gulf of Finland, she could feel it returning. Hanging around a kid certainly was a factor, as was Marcus's invitation. But there was something about the sea itself which invigorated her, felt liberating. The sharpness of the air, the motion of the ship, the vast sky.

She could do this again, she decided. Next time, she wouldn't mind going by herself, either.

With regret, she recognized that a headache was about to start, lurking behind her eyes and the bridge of her nose. Sighing, Lena reluctantly turned to go back inside. She'd forgotten to pack aspirin and would need to visit the ship's small commissary. As she turned away from the railing, she glanced left toward the stern of the ship. And there was Carter.

He stood alone on the topmost deck, staring through a gap in the plexiglass wind shield into the dark water below.

He hadn't yet seen her. She hesitated; should she interrupt him? She didn't want to intrude. Then she noticed that his fists were balled tight, his shoulders high and tense. As she climbed the steps and got closer, she could hear his breath coming out in shuddering pants.

"Hey, Carter. What's up?" His distress was so palpable that she couldn't blithely ignore it.

He just shook his head furiously, never removing his eyes from the sea.

She tried to guess. "Did you have a fight with your folks?"

"I wish I was dead. They wouldn't care. They'd be happy."

Lena caught her breath. She sensed this wasn't an idle threat.

She recalled her own experience at age thirteen with the seductive lure of death: *Everyone will be sorry.* And how much more alluring death seemed when the bitter realization followed: *No one will be sorry. No one will even miss me.* What could her adult self have said to her younger self to dissuade her from attempting suicide? She didn't know. Her younger self had tried it. The rat poisoning had made her so violently ill that her parents had rushed her to the emergency room in time. Her second attempt, at seventeen, was triggered by intense bullying by a group of girls in her language arts class. It was a subject she loved, but she took to skipping the class to avoid them. The teacher had confronted her one day after school and chastised her for missing so much. She'd made the mistake of showing up the next day only to find that the girls had created a cardboard tombstone emblazoned with the words, "Baggy Maggie, RIP. Go kill yourself and set us free." They carried the sign around the school that day, skillfully hiding it when teachers and staff passed by. Enough students saw it, though; she could hear the cruel ditty whispered in her wake in the hallways, the ensuing laughter.

She knew then she had no choice but to die, hence the scar on her wrist. That attempt had failed also.

And she was glad. She was very glad to be alive.

Lena leaned on the railing next to Carter and joined him in studying the sea. "Not a good solution, suicide. It's one of those things you regret the moment you do it."

He looked at her. "You tried?"

"Twice." She pulled up the black leather sleeve, exposing the faint scar. "This was the second time.

The first time was rat poison. Horrible." She shuddered at the memory of the violent cramps and nausea.

"Why did you do it?"

She shrugged, mouth pulling down thoughtfully at the corners. "People are cruel and stupid and afraid of people who aren't like them. I stood out. Too tall, too skinny, too shy. I was an easy target. They made fun of my posture - saggy Maggie - and my clothes - baggy Maggie. When I was seventeen, some mean girls told me to kill myself."

Carter stared at her. "You should have punched them."

"Yes, you're probably right," she smiled ruefully. "I was too afraid to stand up to them. Instead, I tried to oblige."

He stated the obvious. "It didn't work."

"No, it didn't work." She took a deep breath. "I was bleeding into the kitchen sink, realizing how shitty I was to mess it up, that I should have planned things better, when my kid brother came home early. Basketball practice had been canceled. He found me standing there. He didn't say a word, just wrapped my wrist up tightly, sat me down, got me one of his energy drinks. Cleaned things up before our mom got home."

"Was he sad?"

Lena paused, embarrassed at the memory. "He was more mad, really. He still remembered my earlier attempt. That's why he didn't tell my folks. Not to protect me, but to protect them." She took a shaky breath. She hadn't shared this part of the story before, even with her old boyfriend. "I bought him a PlayStation but he wouldn't take it until I told him it was my personal pledge never to try it again."

He whispered, "Did you ever?"

"No. And not just because I'd made a promise. I had learned something important. That I had paid so much attention to girls I hated and who hated me, that I'd forgotten about the people I loved and who loved me. Like my brother." She thought about him in Alaska with his family. Their relationship had never completely healed; another faint scar. Leaning toward Carter, she added, "I'd given my enemies the power to erase me."

Carter was silent. A long moment passed before he said, "I don't have a brother. Or a sister. I only have my parents."

He didn't need to say more. Lena was at a loss. Her own family - to varying degrees - had been supportive. She couldn't imagine Carter's isolation. "Do you want me to talk to them? Tell them how much their comments hurt?"

Carter vehemently burst out. "No! Don't talk to them! It'd only make things worse!"

"Okay, okay," she backed off. Still, she felt she had to offer something. "Do you have any friends at home you trust?"

He nodded slowly. "Stevie. He's a year ahead of me. He's gay. We hang out and play video games."

"Well, that's good. Try talking with Stevie about what you're going through with your parents. He may be dealing with something similar."

"Maybe." Carter sounded doubtful. "His parents are pretty cool."

Lena tried to think of something else to say. "I don't know if this advice sucks, but, when you're around your parents or mean kids at school, try to imagine you're a spy in hostile territory."

"Like Tobias in the *Animorphs*."

She knew the kids' fantasy books about friends with the ability to morph into animals. "So, you like Tobias?" He was the one who had gotten stuck as a red-tailed hawk, if she remembered. She used to read the stories to her niece.

"I wish I could fly away," he said, voice was full of yearning.

Lena nodded; she could see the appeal of shape-shifting. "What I meant, though, is not quite like the Animorphs. You aren't actually becoming an animal."

"Playacting."

"Exactly. Just remember it's only playacting. It's not who you really are. In five or six years, you can leave and find people who accept you, love you, as you are."

"That's a long time."

"Yes," she said sadly. "That is a long time."

They both were silent for several minutes. Then Carter asked, "What did you do? So, you never felt like killing yourself again?"

She exhaled and thought about her answer. "Well, when I was still in high school, I bought vintage black clothes at second-hand stores, and started wearing white makeup, black mascara and eyeliner, black lipstick. If people thought I was weird anyway, I might as well be weird. By then, I'd heard some goth music and liked the lyrics. I basically reinvented myself."

Carter looked puzzled. "How do you do that? Reinvent yourself?"

"I became Lena. When I went to college, I ditched Maggie. It's not a bad nickname but it had too many negative memories for me. And that's when I found the goth community. With them, I finally felt like I belonged."

"But that's not me. I'm not goth."

"Your community is out there, though. Be yourself and you'll find them, I know you will."

Carter turned back to the metallic sea. In the low sun, the sea shone like metal. It would take many hours more before sunset and, even then, the sky would not become completely black, they were that far north.

Watching him, Lena ached. She didn't know how to reach him, how to convince him not to give up on the world, on a happy life. "You know another thing I do? I keep a journal. Do you ever do that?"

Shaking his head, no, the boy kept staring out.

"Journaling works, for me at least. I write to make sense of what's happening around me. Sort of do-it-yourself therapy, you know? Before I had friends to talk to, before I found a therapist I could trust and afford."

"I don't like to write," explained Carter.

"Some people paint, some compose song lyrics. It doesn't have to be written."

"I make recordings sometimes. On my phone."

"That would work," Lena agreed. Then she had another idea. "You can also call me."

"I can?"

"Sure. Let me give you my number."

He handed her his camouflage phone. She typed quickly. "There," she said, handing it back. "My phone and email. In case you need to talk to me." She wondered if he ever would. More likely, she'd never hear from him after the cruise. That realization saddened her a little.

"Thanks," Carter said before lapsing into silence. Suddenly, he blurted out. "I know where I want to go for my birthday tomorrow night. Would you take me?"

"Absolutely."

"There's a group called Friends of Dorothy for LGBT people. They meet in a bar, though. Do you

think you could get me in, since I'm only a kid? Just
to talk to somebody? No offense, but somebody like
me?" The words tumbled out.

Lena started to nod even before he finished
speaking. "No offense taken. I think it's a great idea."

"I'm a boy, not a girl," Carter announced. "I've
never been a girl."

Lena knew this but the boldness of his assertion
pleased her. She recognized it was a statement to
himself as well as to her. "Yes, you're a boy. And
whatever you need, I'm here for you."

Uncertain of her sincerity, he turned to face her
and looked into her eyes. "Really?"

"Really, truly." She could see the tension, the
fear, the caution, drain from his body.

At that moment, a glacial blast blew through the
opening in the wind shield. Carter shivered.

"It's freezing out here," Lena observed, pulling
her own jacket tightly across her chest. "Let's go inside. You can tell me about Tobias and the other Animorphs while we have dessert."

His shoulders relaxed as he settled back into boy-
hood. "Okay," he grinned.

As they headed toward the Galley Buffett entrance, though, he abruptly stopped. "But won't having dessert now spoil my dinner?" he asked her
earnestly.

Lena heard the years of conditioning behind his
question. In her opinion, too many years of too many

rules had boxed him in. Taking his arm and guiding him forward, she decided it was time to loosen those restraints. "Sometimes, Carter, it's okay to eat dessert first."

8

Okay, so I'm starting this journal. It's Lena's idea. She says it's a good way to deal with things in life that are bothering you. Well, she said it worked for her, and thought I could try it.

First big thing. I told Lena I'm a boy. She seems totally okay with it. Stevie knows but no one else. Tomorrow, she's taking me to meet Friends of Dorothy. I'm going to tell them I'm Carter Blue. That's my new last name. Maybe there'll be someone else like me.

<a pause>

This feels weird, talking about myself out loud.

But I have to try this. I really, really don't want to die.

I did earlier. Mom and Dad can be so mean. Sometimes I think they hate me because I'm different. But Lena came by and we talked. She understands a lot. Not everything, but that's okay because she doesn't pretend to know everything. Not like Dad.

And she doesn't try to force me into being a girl, like Mom. She wanted to be a model and now she wants me to be a model and that makes me barf. But she would love me more then, so I don't know what to do.

I told Lena I wish I had a scar on my face. She thought I was joking, and then said maybe I ought to wait until I'm older and see if I still want a scar on my face. I know what I will do, though. I'm going to get a tattoo on my shoulder of a Viking ship sailing away.

I wish I could live with Lena. I wish I could live with her and make a movie for other kids like me. That's another reason I'm doing this journal. It can be like a script. That's why I have to be honest. Lena says that's the most important thing, to be honest with yourself. I need to post it in the cloud, though, with a password so my dad can't get in. I have to protect him and Mom.

I'm going to the gym now. I found it a few days ago. You know, most people don't use it at night. Except for one guy. He's always there. Yesterday he showed me how to use some of the equipment. He said he'd be there tonight and spot me on free weights. I hope so. I need to bulk up. I'm tired of being skinny and small and ... pretty.

So anyway, I'll continue this tomorrow and do it every day and that way I'll have a record of what I was thinking and what I was like as a kid, because Lena says things change a lot after you turn twelve. They can get much better or they can get much worse. Life's a crap shoot, I guess, just like my dad says.

Carter Blue's audio recording 2:29 minutes

9

It was nine-twenty. Lena shifted anxiously in the navy blue Naugahyde chair, turning in expectation each time a new customer arrived at the bar.

Smoothing her black Victorian-style gown, she hoped she looked all right. This was her favorite outfit, with its velvet trim and ruffles on the cuffs. Tonight, she'd opted for dark red lipstick as a contrast. A black velvet fringed shawl was draped over her shoulders. Around her neck, a pearl choker. She touched it lightly. They weren't real pearls; a friend had strung it for her years ago.

Once again, she raised her phone to check the time. Nine-twenty-three.

Sighing, she took another sip of her drink, gloomily conscious that she had been stood up.

Marcus suddenly settled into the seat across the table from her. "Hi, Lena," he said, out of breath. "Sorry I'm late. It took a while to get my father settled down. He kept wanting to talk about Russia."

He came after all. Lena beamed. "I figured it was something like that. Is your dad okay?"

He removed his glasses and massaged the bridge of his nose. Without his glasses, Lena noticed that his eyes were deep set and gray-blue. She liked his look:

tall and moderately fit, with a craggy face and brown hair, wisps of white at the temples.

"He's fine. Took his sleep meds and now he's out until morning. Can I get you something?"

"No, thanks. I'm good." Lena lifted her highball glass, half-full of orangish liquor, ice partially melted.

A cocktail waitress strolled past, and Marcus held up a finger to call her over. "What are you having?" he asked Lena.

"The Drink of the Day: Long Island Iced Tea."

Marcus made a face. "Too sweet for me." Turning to a waitress, he ordered a whisky neat, "George Dickel, if you have it."

The waitress gave a toothy smile. "We have just about everything, sir. Just a minute."

When she left, he shifted his gaze back to Lena. "I appreciated your help today. And the kid's. I was close to the end of my rope, and ... anyway, thanks."

"It was no trouble at all."

"I'm sorry my father got so flirtatious. And the stuff about the KGB. All of that's new." Marcus tightened his mouth, lowered his eyes. "I never thought I'd see him like this. Changing into someone I hardly recognize. He was incredibly sharp. And strict when I was growing up."

Lena could sympathize. "My favorite uncle had Alzheimer's so I know a little about dementia. It's terrible. It can tear a family apart."

"It can," he nodded, then looked up at the waitress as she placed a garden-themed napkin on the table, his whisky on top. "Thanks," he told her.

Watching him taste the whisky, Lena considered something. "Would you like me to take your dad for a while tomorrow, to give you a break? We can walk around the promenade or watch a movie in the ship theater." She had temporarily forgotten her promise to take Carter into Helsinki.

"No," he said. "Thanks anyway. I don't spend enough time with him when we're home. Last year, I moved him into a nearby assisted living facility, so I could visit him more often. But work gets so hectic sometimes, I can miss seeing him for days at a time. I just don't know how much longer before...." He stared across the bar, as if the answer was there. "When he'll stop knowing who I am.... When he'll stop knowing who he is."

The sadness in his voice touching her, she touched the back of his hand. "If you need me to help, let me know."

He spontaneously placed his other hand over hers and squeezed.

Neither spoke. The silence wasn't altogether comfortable, so, as Marcus took another drink, Lena shifted the conversation. "Where's home?"

"Cleveland," he replied. "Three generations. I remember you said you're from L.A."

"Burbank, actually. I write an entertainment column for a local paper and have a music blog." She took another sip of Long Island tea. It was too sweet, she realized. "What do you do in Cleveland?"

"I'm in law enforcement."

He didn't elaborate. She decided to push, just slightly. "What laws do you enforce? Animal, mineral, vegetable?"

For the first time since she had met him, Marcus gave a genuine smile. "Definitely animal. I'm a homicide investigator. On vacation," he emphasized.

"Good thing, too. That means no homicides to investigate, right?"

"I'm counting on it. Are you on vacation, too? Or are you working undercover on your next major entertainment scoop?"

Lena became aware of 1970s pop music in the background and laughed. "What? That Captain and Tennille are alive and well on the Baltic Sea? Don't worry. This is all off the record."

"Good," he said. "My mom loved Captain and Tennille. Let's keep their secret."

They settled back in their seats and Marcus ordered another round of drinks. Conversation was comfortable, wide-ranging, nothing too personal. More than two hours passed, and another round of drinks.

Now was the moment, Lena decided, willing herself to be bold. The three alcoholic drinks helped. She swallowed and plunged in the deep end of the pool. "Would you like to come back to my room?"

Startled, Marcus blinked. "Do you mean to sleep together?"

"Well, yes. Would you like to?" Her heart was starting to sink. Repeating the question was embarrassing. She had obviously misread his signals, and quickly downplayed the importance of her invitation, "Nothing serious, just a shipboard fling."

He didn't reply at first, just stared at his whisky. "Lena, I ...," he paused. "I apologize for giving you the wrong impression. I'm really not looking for.... I mean, my head is in the wrong space right now. For a shipboard fling." He cleared his throat. "Is it okay if we just stay friends?"

"Of course! That was a crazy idea!" Lena forced a laugh, as if she didn't really care at all. But she did. She had never propositioned a man before. She knew now she never would again. The rejection felt too personal: she wasn't attractive, wasn't desirable. She abruptly stood, swaying slightly. "I got to go now."

"Let me walk you back to your place," Marcus stood as well.

"No, no. Stay and finish your drink. I'm okay. I'll see you later," and with a loose wave goodbye to Marcus Vanin, Lena lurched out of the bar.

⚓

Stupid, stupid, stupid, Lena muttered drunk-
enly, angrily, to herself as she stumbled into the mir-
rored elevator and punched fifteen. Her stateroom
was on thirteen, but her finger missed. She slouched
back into the elevator's corner, avoiding the mirror's
dispassionate gaze. She didn't want to see what it
would show.

She'd take the stairs down to her deck, she decided as she stumbled through the elevator doors on
deck fifteen. At the last minute, though, she changed
her mind and continued through the empty Galley
Buffet and out of the automatic glass doors into the
chill wind topside. Pulling the velvet shawl over her
head and around her body, Lena stopped and looked
around. Past midnight and the sky still wasn't fully
dark. A few ominous clouds lay along the horizon but
otherwise it was clear, with a scattering of pale stars.

No one was around. It was too late and too cold.

Lena had no plan other than self-excoriation.
Queasy from too much Long Island Tea and mortified
that she had thrown herself at Marcus, she made her
unsteady way to the portside, hand-over-hand holding on to the deck chairs, weaving toward the glass
enclosure reserved for smokers. Deck chairs lined the
room's edge, the black Baltic waters to their backs.
Unoccupied now.

Good, she thought as she huddled morosely into
a corner seat, long legs drawn up, wrapped in a

cocoon of black velvet. She tried to make herself as small as possible.

Within ten minutes, an alcoholic haze settled over her. Her eyelids drooped; her head fell forward and she briefly dozed.

Something roused her. Before she was fully aware, her head snapped up. Legs were cramping now, her back cold and sore, but she sensed not to move.

A massive shadow passed by the entrance to the smoking enclosure. A bulky man carrying something. It was slightly darker now, and Lena had to squint to see what he held. It's a white plastic bag, like groceries are carried in, she realized. Lena imagined him smuggling an illicit beer or two up for a quiet drink topside, out of sight of the ship's crew. The cruise line assessed a fee on alcohol brought on board by passengers, to encourage consumption of shipboard offerings. The man's furtive movements - head swiveling around; shadowy shoulders high - made Lena suspect he hadn't paid the fee. His beer was contraband. Well, she wasn't going to report him. Let him have his sad party of one, she thought glumly.

He was well past her now, past the unoccupied hot tubs and darkened video arcade, moving with purpose toward the steps to deck sixteen further aft.

Lena's head started to clear from the adrenaline triggered by his appearance. She blinked rapidly and wondered what time it was. "Time to get to bed," she scolded herself. She had to get up early to meet Carter and keep her promise to take him into Helsinki. It was his birthday, after all, and she was ashamed at how quickly she had forgotten that when talking with Marcus.

Marcus. Well, being with Carter would provide a valid reason to avoid the homicide investigator from Cleveland tomorrow. With luck, she could avoid him the rest of the journey.

Lena unraveled her legs, stretched them out and stood. Wrapping the fringed shawl tightly around her shoulders, she quietly made her way back inside.

10

Marcus sat dumbfounded for several minutes after Lena left.

She clearly had had too much to drink. He worried a little about her, wished she had let him walk her back to her stateroom. But he had offended her.

She had offered herself and he had turned her down. He regretted his tone, so peremptory. But it was because she'd surprised him. He wasn't used to getting propositioned. And he really wasn't thinking about sex. Couldn't imagine thinking about it while he was so preoccupied with what was happening to his father.

It wasn't that she didn't attract him. She did, in a way. Admittedly, she wasn't the type of woman who usually drew his eye. She was about as tall as he was, and willowy. And her style was definitely different

But, as he thought about it, he quite liked her. She was kind and intelligent, and felt comfortable enough in her own skin to travel alone. Not everyone could do that, either because they were afraid, or because they couldn't stand their own company. He had always liked his own company, and appreciated that quality in someone else.

Then why hadn't he said yes? It wasn't as if she was asking for a major commitment.

His father, of course. But his father was deep asleep right now. Which made Marcus wonder if his father - or rather, his father's illness - really was the obstacle to intimacy. He hoped not. The doctor had said his father could hang on for another five years, possibly longer. Dementia doesn't travel on a linear path, the doctor had explained. Expect ups and downs for a while, before the downs become more pro-nounced, before there are no more ups.

His father's diagnosis came about the same time as the breakup of his marriage. Was there something to that? He hadn't slept with anyone since then, an irony given that the marriage had ended because of his infidelity. Maybe that explained why he lived now as a penitent.

Well, his marriage had actually ended before that. His wife had moved out of the house four months earlier; she'd gotten fed up with his long hours away, his morose and sullen moods when he was home.

He hadn't always been that way. For most of his career in the Division of Police, he'd balanced just at the edge of hope. Sure, people were killing people, brutally, sometimes incomprehensibly. But he was good at catching killers and knew he was making a difference, making his city safer. For ten years, hom-icides rates had plummeted; in just three of those

years, they had fallen by half. Recently, though, hom-
icides had started to soar again, whiplashing back to
the bad old days. It wasn't just in Cleveland either.

How can you stanch that bloody tide? Tide, hell;
it was a tsunami, and it carried the flotsam of whatever optimism he once had felt.

Maybe he needed a new line of work, although he
couldn't imagine what it would be. Something to
think about when he got home.

Agitated with himself, disgusted at his hesitation
with Lena, Marcus tossed back the rest of his whisky
and left the bar. Tomorrow, he told himself, he'd look
for her and see if she was still interested.

11

The woman known as Aurora was euphoric. Suppressing the desire to skip down the passageway, she maintained a pace more suitable to an affluent middle-aged widow. But once inside her stateroom, away from other passengers, the steward and the omnipresent CCTV cameras, she burst into laughter. Gales of laughter. The Masseks were so gullible! To be honest, though, she had to give herself credit for being an exceptional actor.

She'd had a moment's doubt about success when the kid had refused to go with her into St. Petersburg. She intended to use the day trip to build trust. But that didn't matter now. She could count on dear Janelle and Jay to pave the way for success in Stockholm.

After kicking off the four-inch heels, Aurora looked in the mirror and winked at the attractive plump woman. It was time to change out of Kellie Rose Roberts, her stage name in this little drama.

First, she pulled out from her upper lip the silicon device that subtly changed the shape of her mouth. Useful both because it interfered with facial recognition software, and, importantly, it made her less attractive; people were wary around the beautiful, and she needed people to trust her. Aurora stretched her lips and moved her jaw. What a relief to get that thing out, she thought. Then she carefully removed the curly auburn wig, unpinned her shoulder-length brown hair and massaged her scalp. Discarding the tortoise shell eyeglasses, she popped out the green colored contact lenses that transformed her blue eyes. Then came off the well-crafted fake diamond earrings and the equally tasteful fake diamond ring.

Aurora quickly undressed: the black pantsuit and white silk blouse, the heavily padded bra, the layers of fabric padding that thickened her torso and added thirty pounds to her silhouette. She was almost finished, almost herself again. All she needed was a shower to scrub off the rose-peach makeup, reclaiming her olive complexion.

She knew how memory worked. The Masseks and others would only remember certain things about her appearance: false impressions of her hair and eye color, skin tone, weight and height. Her image on the ship's security cameras should be sufficiently distorted with the mouth piece and glasses, but it wouldn't matter anyway. Even with a perfect photo, they wouldn't be able to find Kellie Rose Roberts. They'd find a real woman in Boston by that name, and a fake Facebook account that Aurora had set up months before in case inquisitive parents tried to check up on her. After this affair, it was time for Kellie Rose to disappear for good, Aurora decided.

Under the hot water now, she replayed the evening's success: how grateful the parents were with her promised financial assistance. How relieved they were that more support might be coming. And how delighted they were when they learned that Kellie Rose was friends with the associate director of the famous Vasa Museum, and that she would arrange for their child to have a personal tour of the famous ship. Cautioning them not to trust strangers too much, she had even placed a call to her friend, the "associate director," so they could receive his personal assurances that their child would be safe. Getting off in Nynäshamn, fifty-eight kilometers south of Stockholm, would pose no problems, she knew. Security was relaxed and there would be no passport checks as they entered Sweden. A taxi would be waiting for them, she had told the Masseks; they'd go straight to the museum, get lunch in the café there, and be back to the ship in time for the four o'clock departure.

She had talked up the Vasa Museum, but not too much. She didn't want Jay and Janelle to decide to come along; in fact, that was the last thing she wanted. Instead, with the parents' blessing, she'd get the child off the ship and they'd drive away. And neither would be heard from again.

In about thirty-two hours, it would be over, the easiest kidnapping of her career.

Aurora wasn't deterred by the fact that Jennifer - or Carter, if she preferred - distrusted her. All she had to do that morning was slip a little hyoscine hydrobromide into whatever the kid was drinking. Not too much; Aurora didn't want to poison her. The right amount, however, would make Carter not just pliable but highly susceptible to her suggestions. Down in Colombia, Aurora had heard that new mothers under its influence could even be convinced by adoption traffickers to give up their babies. The best part of the drug was the memory loss; even years from now, the kid wouldn't remember how she had been taken, or by whom.

Aurora was also pleased that she could avoid working with Eddie, could cut him out of the deal completely. He was too unreliable, erratic, even. And rude. She'd already spoken with Management about him, and they agreed with her plan. Eddie just wasn't necessary.

They also were intrigued by her recommendation of customer. She knew someone who would pay top dollar for a child like Jennifer: with both an extraordinary feminine beauty and the behavior and sensibilities of a boy. Too bad she was turning twelve. Well, she was small enough that she could pass for ten, even nine, if Management thought that was necessary. Aurora didn't think it would be. The child embodied so many sexually enticing qualities that age would not be a stumbling block to a sale. Hey, there might even be a bidding war for her.

That notion thrilled Aurora. She did it for the money, of course. But she also loved the game.

12

A hangover headache assaulted Lena before she'd even opened her eyes. She remembered now that she'd forgotten to buy more aspirin yesterday, after the intense conversation with Carter. And then, of course, she'd been diverted by drinks with Marcus. Marcus. She groaned as she remembered how she had thrown herself at him. She wanted to hide in bed.

What time was it, anyway? She peeked at the stateroom's clock, almost blinded by the light already streaming in from the partially open shades. Squeezed her eyes shut again. Six thirty-five. She had to get going. Lena groaned again and rolled off the king bed, found her slippers and staggered into the bathroom. She fought the persistent urge to crawl back between the sheets.

She was supposed to meet Carter for breakfast at seven. That way, they could be among the first to disembark, before everyone else on the Sea Dream converged on Helsinki. There wasn't an organized shore excursion today, but the Passenger Service Desk had told her to follow a painted green line to the tram station; then take number nine to the city's Art Deco train station. From there, they could wander around downtown, visit Senate Square, with its Parliament

House and neoclassical Cathedral, then leisurely make their way to the famous Market Square for reindeer sausage. Carter had insisted on tasting reindeer. Along the way, she'd find a gift for him. Something special.

We must be getting close, she thought as she brushed her hair, and opened the balcony door to watch the approaching shore line. A seagull – white-bellied and gray-winged – swooped screaming near her head. Lena jerked back, falling heavily into the plastic chair on the balcony. "Damn bird," she muttered. At least it woke her up.

Twenty minutes later, she had showered and dressed and found a table on the port side of the Galley Buffet. Carter wasn't there yet, so she sat facing the entrance to watch for him as she ate. Seven came and went. When he didn't appear by seven-fifteen, she began to wonder if he had changed his mind. Perhaps his parents had planned something else that day. She hoped not. Then she reproached herself. She actually hoped they did. He needed his parents' attention; he was hungry for it.

By seven-twenty, breakfast finished, she decided to look for him. She couldn't sit there all morning.

First, she tried the disembarkation point, but he wasn't waiting in line. Since his other likely haunt, the video arcade, wasn't open yet, she decided to check his parents' stateroom. Their suite number was easy to remember. Getting access, however, was another matter; it was in one of the exclusive areas of the ship, where Lena's key card didn't work. She hung around the area's entrance for a few minutes and then, in luck, noticed an elderly man heading toward it. He swiped his key card, and she held the heavy door open for him. After he thanked her, she slipped in behind him. In a few minutes, she was at the door to the Masseks' suite.

She knocked. With no immediate response, she knocked again, slightly harder. Just as she was about to turn away, the door opened and there stood a disheveled Janelle. Lena recognized her from the castle in Estonia.

"Good morning. I'm Lena Albright, a friend of Carter's. We're supposed to go into Helsinki today, and I'm just checking to see if he's still able to go."

"First off," the woman said gruffly and then coughed. "Her name is Jennifer. I know she likes to play at being a boy but she's a girl. And second," another smoker's morning cough interrupted, longer this time. "And second, she's sleeping in. It is, after all, her birthday." Janelle motioned toward a lump under a pile of blankets on the sofa. To the right, Lena saw a half-opened door to the master bedroom.

Lena knew from Carter that his parents didn't accept him, but she still was surprised at the depth of Janelle's denial. As if Carter was simply pretending to be a boy to aggravate her.

"Can I at least wish him... her... a happy birth-day?" Lena asked, staying in the doorway. He deserved at least one genuine birthday wish. Then she would leave.

Janelle, sighing melodramatically, shuffled to the sofa, rustled the covers, and called Jennifer's name. Suddenly, she threw back the blanket and cried out, "What the hell?!"

Lena was instantly beside her. Carter's father Jay rushed from the bedroom a second later.

There was no child.

13

"She's gone! It's her birthday, and she's supposed to be here!" Janelle wheeled on Lena. "Where is she?! What have you done with her?!"

Lena took a step back. "I don't know. That's why I came by." She thought about adding the word 'bitch' but decided it was too harsh. Maybe that's what mothers did when their children went missing; they blamed others.

Jay spoke calmly but firmly to Lena. "Did you see her at breakfast? The video arcade? The disembarkation area?" She shook her head no to each inquiry.

"Oh, God," Janelle panicked. "You don't think she went into Helsinki on her own?"

Jay picked up the phone.

"Who the hell are you call...?" Janelle started to ask, but he held up his hand to silence her.

"Ship Security? Our daughter is missing and we'll need your help to locate her. Yes, we're in the Sanctuary, suite eighty."

Within five minutes, a security officer was there with the news that their daughter had not left the ship. He wrote down Jennifer's height and weight, and uploaded Janelle's photos. Then he alerted crew and other officers to start the search of the ship's public areas, kitchens, laundry, and other work spaces that the child might have found unlocked and accessible.

Within eight minutes, security guards on duty the night before had reported that they had seen nothing unusual.

When Jennifer was still not found, the officer at the Masseks got a call that all the crew's quarters were being searched as well, just in case. The tension in the room thickened. Janelle started to hyperventilate; Jay put his arm around her. Neither said anything to Lena.

Then came a brisk knock on the Masseks' door. Two men entered, one of them Marcus. Lena was momentarily shocked to see him there. He didn't seem surprised to see her.

The unknown man spoke first, shaking first Jay and then Janelle's hands. "Good morning," he said. "I'm Chief Security Officer James Bronson. I want to reassure you that we will find Jennifer. We are using every resource at our disposal. This is Detective Vanin of the Cleveland Police Department. He has kindly agreed to assist in our inquiries."

"Good morning, Lena," Marcus said.

Avoiding his gaze, she nodded in acknowledgment.

Jay and Janelle were guided to the still untidy sofa. Before sitting, Janelle picked up the blankets and dropped them on the floor by the balcony door for the steward to collect later. Bronson and Marcus settled into chairs across from them, but Lena stayed leaning against the built-in desk.

Extricating a notebook and pen from his jacket, Bronson asked, "What was Jennifer wearing when you last saw her?"

"Jeans and polo shirt," Janelle said, distracted. "She likes polo shirts." The security chief looked expectantly at her but she didn't elaborate.

"It's forest green, with long sleeves." Lena broke in, realizing that details might matter. "The polo shirt. And possibly a tan windbreaker. On the shirt's right chest, there's an insignia of the clothing brand. I don't remember which one."

Bronson scribbled in his notebook, then looked at the parents. "We've got people culling through the ship's CCTV cameras, but that could take a while. We can speed up the process if we know more about her movements last night. When and where did you last see your daughter?"

Jay took charge. "She came in soon after seven-thirty. The four of us left for dinner just before eight. We went to Chez Pierre, the French restaurant. You can check."

"The four of you?" Marcus interrupted.

"My wife and I, Jennifer and a friend of ours."

Marcus followed up. "Your friend's name?"

"I don't see how that's relevant," Jay said, but grudgingly added, "It was another passenger. Mrs. Kellie Rose Roberts."

"Was Jennifer with you the whole evening?" Bronson asked.

"No. She left. I couldn't say when exactly," Jay said. "It was after we finished eating."

"A little after nine," Janelle explained.

"That's right," Jay recalled. "A little after nine."

Marcus interrupted. "How long after nine? Two minutes, twenty?"

Jay looked at his wife. She responded, "Five minutes after nine, I guess. Jennifer stood up from the table at nine. She wanted to get back to the room, so I brought her back here, then returned to my husband and our friend."

"Any particular reason she wanted to get back?" Bronson queried. "Was she meeting someone? Did she have any plans?"

Janelle snorted. "She couldn't stand being out with us. How's that for a reason?"

"Our daughter is a typical moody twelve-year-old," Jay asserted, unconsciously echoing Kellie Rose's observation from the night before. Then he continued. "We stayed out another two hours, talking with Mrs. Roberts. Got back here at eleven or so. When we saw the pile of bedding on the sofa, we assumed it was Jennifer sleeping, so we retired to our bedroom, quietly talked over business plans and had another drink to celebrate our good fortune."

"Good fortune," a sob catching in Janelle's throat.

"And the good fortune is?" Marcus left the question open.

"Mrs. Roberts is investing in my business," Jay answered curtly. "Though I still don't see how that's relevant to Jennifer's disappearance."

Bronson explained as he made notes, "We'll be focusing on the hall cameras, the restaurant, adjacent elevators and stairways from nine o'clock onward." He didn't tell them that another officer was interviewing the steward, and his account would be compared with the Masseks'.

"We only discovered Jennifer was missing when that woman showed up this morning." Jay motioned toward Lena.

Bronson turned his gaze to her. "And who are you?"

"Lena Albright. I'm a friend of Cart.... Jennifer's. We were going into Helsinki today, but when she didn't show up at breakfast, I stopped by to see if she was all right."

"Is there any reason to believe that she might not be all right?" Marcus broke in.

She understood what he was really asking; after all, he now knew Carter's secret. Lena kept her expression neutral. "No, none. I thought she might not be feeling well. Or, maybe, since it's her birthday, her parents had something special planned."

"We did," Janelle hissed fiercely.

"When was the last time you saw her?" Bronson ignored the interruption.

"A little before seven-thirty last night. Before she returned here for dinner."

"Just in passing?"

Lena had to think about this, how much to reveal about their conversation. This was the time to mention the talk of suicide, but she didn't. She worried it would divert their attention from a search of the ship. "We chatted for an hour or so up on the deck. Looking out at the sea."

"Chatting about anything in particular?" Marcus probed.

Lena again discounted answering truthfully. "About the trip so far," she lied.

"Any communication after that?"

Lena shook her head no. She remembered something that might be useful, though. "Jennifer told me she liked to go to the ship's fitness center in the evenings."

"The fitness center," Bronson noted. "Easy to check. Key cards are needed for entry after eight." He made a call.

"How did she seem to you last night, Lena?" Marcus leaned toward her.

Lena knew he was pushing her to expose Carter's secret to his parents, and she resented it. Yet, with Marcus involved in the case, she couldn't deny it either, even if she didn't believe it was germane to Carter's disappearance. She chose her words carefully. "Last night, Jennifer - who prefers to be called Carter - told me that she is a boy born in a girl's body. She seemed relieved to be able to talk about it."

She could hear Bronson softly say, "transgender boy" as he made notes. It wasn't the shocking revelation it would have been even a few years earlier.

From the corner of her eye, she could see Jay and Janelle's furious faces. Jay stood to speak, but before he could, Marcus pressed further. "She didn't seem depressed or upset about anything?"

Lena briefly considered how to answer. "No. We made plans to go into Helsinki today. And she asked especially if I would go with her to a meeting of Friends of Dorothy on board this evening. She was looking forward to that."

Bronson asked, "The child had not met anyone from this group earlier?"

"No." Lena amended herself, "Not to my knowledge."

The Chief scribbled a reminder to interview some of the regular participants, in case they knew of Jennifer's whereabouts.

Bronson's phone beeped. The child's keycard had been used to access the ship's gym at nine-forty, he reported. And there was something else. He turned to Jay and Janelle, "At five this morning, one of the crew found a child's pair of athletic shoes on deck sixteen, the upper deck. Are your daughter's shoes missing?"

Janelle quickly checked the closet. "What color are they? The ones they found?"

Lena was touched by the agony in her voice.

"Black with yellow markings."

"Oh, God," Janelle fell heavily on the sofa next to Jay.

Bronson leaned toward them. "We need to explore the possibility that your child fell overboard last night," he said gently. "In addition to our other efforts, we'll ask ships in the vicinity of the most likely area to conduct a search. Once again, anything you may remember about her movements last night could help us narrow the search area and find her more quickly."

"Jumped?!" Janelle wailed. Jay didn't even respond. Stone-faced and stoic, he barely blinked.

"Or an accident," the Chief quickly added. "Or she's still on board. We haven't given up finding her this morning."

"She didn't jump," Lena ventured. The words came out before she consciously thought about it, but they felt true nonetheless. Carter committing suicide would have contradicted everything she felt they'd established yesterday, and all of their planning for the future. It couldn't be true.

Quickly, Janelle turned on her. "What do you know about my daughter?" Her voice rising, she shouted, "Get out!"

Marcus stepped between Janelle and Lena, and spoke softly, "Lena, why don't you wait for me in your stateroom. I'll meet you in about an hour and we can finish the interview there."

14

What could have happened to him? Lena brooded as she left the Masseks' stateroom. Where was he? She didn't think he had run away. More likely that he was stuck somewhere, injured or held against his will.

Instead of returning to her room, she stopped by the business center, tucked away near the commissary. Using a photo of him she'd taken the day before, she constructed a flier:

HAVE YOU SEEN ME?
Boy, blond hair, hazel eyes, about 4' tall, slender.
Missing since Sunday night after 9:40 p.m.
Wearing tan windbreaker, green shirt and jeans
If you have any information, contact Ship Security
immediately!

She listed the security office's phone number.

Lena knew that identifying Carter as a boy would upset the parents, but that's how other passengers would have seen him. He also didn't look twelve, so she didn't include his age.

With a hundred copies on pale yellow paper, Lena taped up the fliers in the stairwells, the elevators fore and aft, in the video arcade and along the hallways on each residential deck; then she placed them on tables and sofas in the lounges and movie hall.

Where was the gym, she wondered? She'd leave some there as well.

Suddenly, she remembered Marcus and her interview. She was late. Clutching the last two dozen fliers, she ran up the stairs to her stateroom. Marcus would know what to do, she was sure of it.

Lena found him waiting in the corridor. "Hi, I've just printed these out," she said in a rush, handing him a flier. Then she unlocked the door and he followed her in. Marcus in her room at last, Lena thought, but not the way she had imagined it.

He scanned the flier, absorbing it more than reading. "You put these around the ship?"

"Yes. Someone may know something. We've got to act fast."

Marcus frowned. "Lena, she's not going to be found. Please, don't get your hopes up. This isn't a milk carton case. I'm sorry but it's true."

What was he saying? Lena stared at him. "Carter didn't kill himself," she stated flatly and sat on the sofa. She wasn't sure any more that Marcus was going to help.

He glanced toward the bed, then pulled the desk chair over to sit on. He leaned toward her, elbows on knees. "You think someone murdered her? Threw her overboard?"

"No, no," she said. "But he could be hurt somewhere. He might have been kidnapped."

Marcus sighed. "As a trans youth, she was at elevated risk of suicide. That's just a fact."

"You've already decided it's a suicide, haven't you? You're supposed to keep an open mind during an investigation."

He gave her a sharp look. "This isn't my investigation, so I don't have to keep an open mind. That's Chief Bronson's job. My gut instinct tells me that she took her own life. I hope I'm wrong."

"Well, my gut instinct tells me that he didn't and he's still alive," Lena retorted. The more she thought about it, the more convinced she became that she was right.

Marcus didn't reply.

His insistence on referring to the child as a girl exasperated Lena. This battle over pronouns felt personal, a tug of war with Carter's body. He didn't see himself as a girl; why should she? To Lena, Carter always was a boy and she wasn't going to capitulate.

But that was a minor point if they didn't find him soon. "He can't have killed himself, Marcus. Last night, we made plans for his birthday. He was happy. You saw him, too, when we came back from St. Petersburg. Did he seem depressed to you? Suicidal?"

Leaning back and crossing his arms, Marcus studied her. "No. But a lot can change for a kid in a few hours. I've seen it in a dozen cases where normal-seeming kids later do things that hurt themselves or others. People around them miss the clues."

"And we missed the clues? Is that what you're saying?" Lena didn't want to show it, but his remark struck her; she raced back through her memory for a sign she might have missed.

"His parents aren't exactly supportive." Marcus caught himself then. "*Her* parents, I mean." He wasn't going to yield on the pronoun either.

She couldn't help herself; she had to confront him. "Why are you doing that? Why are you denying Carter's identity by referring to him as a girl?"

"Because the kid hasn't - hadn't - transitioned yet. In fact, other than to you and me, I don't think she - or he - posed as a boy to anyone else."

This irritated her. "He wasn't posing. Of that much I'm sure."

Marcus groaned. "You know what I mean. What I'm trying to say is that Carter had cause to be depressed. At best, the Masseks are - were - disinterested parents. He probably embarrassed them, or disappointed their dreams for their beautiful daughter. They told me, when Jennifer was little, they ascribed her behavior to being a tomboy. When she turned ten, they started to insist she dress and act *normally* at home. Their word, not mine. On cruises, though, they left her alone. They called it indulging her *quirk*. At sea, no one knew them. It couldn't hurt the father's business or the mother's social standing. The cruise ends in a few days in Copenhagen. The thought of returning to his old life for another year of bullying at school and hostility at home could have sent the child over the edge." He paused. "He had motive, Lena. You know he did."

She was silent, thinking back to Carter's argument with his parents; his talk of dying. Marcus was close to convincing her, close to shattering her hopes.

Uncomfortable with her silence, he continued. "What evidence do you have that it's not a suicide? Other than wishful thinking?" He said it gently this time, aware that he, too, wished it wasn't so.

Less confident now, Lena spoke softly. "His excitement at meeting the LGBT group tonight, seeing the Vasa ship in Stockholm tomorrow." She met Marcus's gaze. "He had plans. Things to look forward to. He even talked about moving to southern California when he turns eighteen."

"You live there," Marcus observed, remembering.

Lena nodded. "I was outside on deck fifteen last night, not far from the stairway to sixteen. I was there from twelve-something until past one, and Carter didn't pass by."

She dreaded him following up to ask why she had been outside at that hour, but he didn't.

"That doesn't mean he wasn't there at eleven or one-thirty or three," Marcus noted. He leaned toward her. "I think you're blaming yourself for not being up there when he went by. Maybe you think that, if you had been, he wouldn't have jumped. It's not your fault, Lena." He lightly touched her knee in sympathy.

Some of what he said was true, that Lena partly did blame herself for whatever bad was happening to the boy. Especially if Marcus was right and Carter had taken his own life. "But he had plans," she repeated. She needed to believe that was important. She looked at Marcus, also less accusatory in her tone. "And you? What makes you so sure it's suicide? Other than generic studies about gender dysphoria?"

He didn't want to lay out the evidence. It wasn't his case. He was merely consulting, and didn't know what he should share. Yet involving Lena might be productive; she might remember something Carter said or did. Besides, he didn't want her telling other passengers that the child had been kidnapped. The flier was a case in point; it unnecessarily alarmed every parent on board. He had to get her to see how her belief was unfounded. He had to get her to leave the investigation to the professionals.

"To start with, the CCTV cameras. Security found video..."

Lena leaned forward. "You saw the footage from the fitness center?"

"I didn't but security personnel did. Unfortu-
nately, those two cameras have been acting up for the
past few days. Sometimes working, sometimes not.
There's only sporadic footage."

Her skepticism was returning. "That seems sus-
pici..."

Marcus talked over her. "Evidently, that's not
unusual, Lena. The entire CCTV system is scheduled
to be replaced next month."

"Sounds too convenient to me."

Ignoring her observation, Marcus continued, "As
I was saying, security officers did find video of someone who appeared to be Carter in a large group of
adult partiers who climbed the stairs to deck sixteen
about ten last night. There's no clear footage showing
that he came down again, either with the group or on
his own. Security has checked the feed from both
sides of the ship. Now they're trying to identify the
adults in the group."

She frowned. "Wait. The video shows someone
who looked like him?"

"Short stature, slender, blond hair. Light-colored
windbreaker and jeans, just as you describe him
here." Marcus held up the yellow flier.

It still might not be Carter, she told herself. She
made the case to Marcus. "That could be any one of
hundreds of people on this ship," she asserted. "And,
even if it was him, he could have been hidden by the

rest of the group when he came back down the stairs. It doesn't mean he jumped."

He plowed on, "Then there's the location on deck sixteen where he likely went into the water - jumped or fell or was pushed. It's out of range of security cameras, which reflects some planning...."

"But," she started to say.

"His shoes were found nearby," Marcus stressed. "And there are suspicious fingerprints on the railing."

Lena grasped at another slender reed of hope. "Suspicious? You're not sure the prints are his."

He was getting a little exasperated with the questioning. "I'm pretty damn sure. The fact that the prints aren't clear can be easily explained: The top of the railing is wood, which isn't as clear of a surface as metal, there was a hard rain at three this morning, and children's hands usually don't have as much oil as adult hands."

"That sounds to me like reasons to ignore those prints. And, besides, how many people walked by that area before the crew cordoned it off?"

Marcus didn't answer. He had to admit it was a faulty crime scene.

She continued. "Did you find his phone?"

"No, we assume it was with him when he...."

Lena could easily challenge this. "If he intended to kill himself – which I don't believe - he would have left it somewhere with a recorded suicide note. He likes recording things on his phone."

She was probably right that it had the suicide note, Marcus thought. He reminded himself to tell the security chief about the cell phone.

"Do you have any other evidence?" Lena pressed.

"Well, the missing weights."

"Missing weights?"

"From the weight room. Two free-weights are missing. Consistent with someone lightweight trying to drown, needing the extra pounds to sink. We already know he accessed the gym. And, to confirm it, that's where we found his jacket."

"His jacket?" This made her pause. "That's unusual, don't you think? It was freezing last night. If he went outside, he would have been wearing his jacket."

"Not necessarily. Not if he was preoccupied with jumping."

Lena suddenly stood. "Show me the spot, Marcus. Please. I need to see it."

He sighed heavily. "All right. But don't touch anything."

15

Janelle sat listlessly at the dressing table. "I have to get ready," she informed herself. "People are coming soon." She had heard Jay on the phone, reaching out to those they had met on board, somberly sharing the news of Jennifer's disappearance. First one, and another, and then most of them said they would be coming by to offer support. With a tragedy, casual acquaintances had become friends, just that quickly.

"What's that, honey?" Jay called from the living room where he was watching television to pass the time. "Did you say something?"

"No, sugar," she called back. Then, to herself, mumbled again. "I've got to get ready."

She tried touching her lips with the fine brush of her lipstick, but she couldn't control her hand. Instead, she picked up the boar bristle brush and passed a few strokes through her blond hair. And then froze, tears streaming down her face.

Brushing hurt too much, reminding her of brushing Jennifer's hair when she was small, no more than four years old. Such gorgeous soft curls, Janelle remembered. She hadn't cut Jennifer's hair until she was six, and only then because Jennifer had hacked off a good chunk with the kitchen shears. Janelle had cried then, too. But Jay had reminded her that children are their own people; that she had to let Jennifer develop in her own way. Within reason, of course.

Jay's mother had begged him to become a concert pianist, but at fifteen he had walked away from the piano forever. He wanted to play sports, study business, be a financial success. Live the good life.

At that time, his point of view made sense. They were living the good life. But his business had taken a hit recently. Where the good life now?

Janelle breathed deeply. She shouldn't have given up her career in modeling. She'd mostly had local gigs with some regional attention, but the agency had really liked her, said she had prospects. If she'd stayed in the profession, she could be bringing some real money into the household. Instead, when she was nineteen, she had met dashing, charming Jay. And all thoughts of being a model went out the window.

Modeling had helped in other ways, though. She knew how to keep up her appearance and play the hostess at Jay's business dinners. After a brief respite when she was pregnant, she was out in the trenches again as soon as Jennifer was born. Then she discovered – quite by accident – that their church was holding a Mother/Baby beauty pageant. She and Jennifer signed up and were the top winning duo. They went on to other competitions, and then she enrolled

Jennifer in toddler pageants. Jennifer simply could not lose. So many trophies! Everyone fell in love with her little girl.

Then came that awful temper tantrum during the formal wear segment of the Petite Miss Pageant, and Janelle, mortified, had had to hurry Jennifer off the stage. She was four then; and from that moment, she'd escalated her outrages, stopping Janelle from entering her again. You can't win a pageant with your face all ugly with tears, she had tried to explain to Jennifer. But Jennifer didn't care.

That was the first time that Jay told her to let Jennifer be herself. Janelle had argued with him: what do children know about what's best for them? Beauty competitions weren't hurting her and, in fact, could build poise and confidence, and lead to more and more success in life, college scholarships, even.

It didn't matter. The older Jennifer got, the more headstrong. Janelle blamed Jay for being gone so much with work; he should have been around more, so they could have presented a united front.

Now their darling girl was gone. Janelle's brush clattered to the dressing table as she buried her face in her hands. No one said it out loud, but you don't jump into cold water from sixteen stories up and survive. Not this long, anyway.

Maybe it was an accident. She wanted to believe it. She could imagine Jennifer standing on top of the railing, holding on to the wind breaks, pretending to be a pirate. It was the kind of stupid and reckless thing she did. Like trying to outrace her father's car. Like climbing on the roof when the air conditioning guys left the ladder out. Like beating up that boy in first grade.

That memory stopped her and triggered other recollections: Jennifer at eight shoving her older cousin; just last year, yelling at neighborhood girls. Janelle had a sudden sick realization: Jennifer had been mentally ill. How else to explain the aggressive, anti-social behavior? She should have taken her daughter to see a therapist; Jennifer had needed help. But she hadn't paid attention and now it was too late.

Janelle broke into wrenching sobs.

In seven minutes, she was finally able to stop. She blotted the tears with tissue paper, daubed concealer and fresh makeup on her reddened nose, picked up her lipstick brush and started again. "People will be coming soon," she whispered, her chest heaving. She had to get ready.

16

Marcus led Lena up to the promenade on deck fifteen and past the swimming, the hot tubs, the outdoor bar. Popular hangouts on the Caribbean cruises but largely neglected in the northern air. As they passed the video arcade, now full of young people, Lena peered inside, just in case Carter was magically there. He wasn't.

Straight down the deck from the glassed-in smoking area was the aft stairway to a small top deck. They climbed it and stopped just where the steps ended. Here, a gap opened between the plexiglass wind shield on the stairway and the one on the upper deck. Wide enough for someone thin to slip through.

Lena stopped in instant recognition. This same spot on the starboard side was where she had encountered Carter the previous evening.

Marcus lifted the yellow crime tape and waited. Unnerved, she hesitated to bend under it. A moment passed before she joined him at the polished wood railing. Hugging herself so she wouldn't inadvertently touch the wood, she peered over the side and noticed that the string of life boats had ended. A jumper here would drop directly into the sea.

Lena couldn't help herself. She imagined Carter sitting on the railing, dangling his legs over the side, staring into the abyss. Or, using the wind shields to either side for balance, standing on the varnished wood, poised to swan dive to his death. She swallowed, bleakly wondering if her instincts were wrong.

Gesturing toward the plexiglass, she asked in a faint voice, "You checked these for prints?

Marcus nodded. "Nothing," he said, then pointed toward a stack of deck chairs still lashed together from the night before. "One of the crew found his shoes there at five this morning. They were damp, which means they were left out before or during the storm that blew through at three."

She shook her head to clear the creeping doubt. She needed to return to her earlier line of questioning, challenging the evidence for suicide. "What do the missing weights look like?"

He shrugged. "Ten-pound barbells. Why?"

They were heavier and differently shaped than she'd imagined. "I don't think he used them," she said, tentatively. In a stronger voice, she added, "Someone else must have taken them."

"According to a crew member who checked the gym at seven-thirty last night, no weights were missing."

Lena started to develop a theory. "Consider this, Marcus. Our kidnapper wants us to think Carter's dead so we'll stop looking for him. And the weights and shoes are props to make it look like suicide."

He shook his head in bewilderment. "You're grasping at straws."

"Barbells don't make sense, though." She had an idea. "Get on the railing as if you were going to jump."

Marcus moved to an area outside the crime tape, in case further prints could be coached from the surface. He quickly hoisted himself up, sat for a second on the railing and dropped back to the deck.

"Carter's not even four and a half feet tall. There is no way he could clamor up the railing with only one hand. He'd need both, just like you did. How could he have carried two ten-pound barbells with him?"

"He probably laid them on the railing, picked them up once he was sitting at the top."

"You checked to see if similar weights would balance on the railing?"

"They would, if he was careful about it." Marcus wasn't giving ground. "Or he could have put them in his pockets while he climbed."

"Sure, if he had his jacket. But he didn't. If he was carrying weights, why leave the jacket behind?"

"He was a depressed and distraught kid. He wasn't thinking straight."

Lena couldn't argue with that; before her own suicide attempts, she certainly hadn't been thinking straight. She recalled the shame at seeing her bright red blood staining the kitchen sink, the place where her mother rinsed vegetables.

Marcus conjectured, "And he could have used his pants pockets."

This theory was so absurd that Lena almost laughed. "He wears skinny kid jeans. There's no way a barbell - even a baby weight - would fit in a pocket. Test it; his mom will have another pair."

Crossing her arms, she felt increasingly emboldened by what she saw as meager evidence for a suicide. She summed it up. "Camera footage: inconclusive. Fingerprints: nothing definitive. Weights: not likely. Jacket: found far away from the supposed jump site. Beloved phone: missing. Suicide note: nada. Shoes. When it comes down to it, all you have are his shoes. And, you know what, someone could have put them there. Someone who wants us to think that Carter's dead. Someone who - for his or her own reasons - wants Carter alive."

"And I suppose you have a suspect," Marcus sighed, glancing at his watch. Lena didn't notice that he was no longer paying serious attention.

She hadn't considered it until he asked, but with sudden clarity, Lena knew. "Carter said he was being followed - stalked, is the word he used - by that great friend of his parents', Kellie Rose Roberts. She could have kidnapped him."

Marcus looked incredulous. "And why would she do that? I met her this morning at the Masseks' stateroom. She's a rich middle-aged woman. Where's her motive?"

"Well, maybe she never had her own children and she's desperate for a child of her own." Lena tried to imagine Kellie Rose as a mother wannabe, but the image didn't quite fit. Ignoring Marcus's growing impatience, she plowed on. "Or she's a pedophile. Or, or she isn't really a rich middle-aged woman but a child trafficker who plans to sell him!" The words alarmed her even as she spoke. "Listen to me, Marcus, Carter's in serious danger!"

"Lena..." He shook his head. "You know how preposterous that sounds."

"Please, Marcus, at least search her room!"

"I've got to go." He passed her a scribbled note. "Here's the phone number in my room if anything else occurs to you. But no more wild accusations about Kellie Roberts. Am I clear?"

"Marcus!"

"Goodbye, Lena."

17

Lena wasn't easily dissuaded. Certainly not by Marcus, not after last night. He dismissed her then, but he wasn't going to dismiss her now, not when it involved Carter. For one thing, she hadn't forgiven him yet for rejecting her; she didn't dwell on the unfairness of it, that he had a right not to be attracted to her. For another thing, she trusted her instincts, and they told her that Kellie Rose Roberts had Carter, whether or not Marcus and Ship Security believed it.

Lena had to get them to search the woman's room. If she couldn't persuade them, the Masseks could. All she had to do was persuade the Masseks.

This time, getting through the security door into the Sanctuary wasn't difficult, with the comings and goings of the Masseks' shipboard acquaintances, ship personnel and security. Through their open stateroom door, Lena saw a security officer talking with the Masseks. Jay was wearing an olive polo shirt and tan slacks; Janelle was in deep pink. Lena hoped that meant they hadn't given up faith that Carter could be found.

Janelle was clutching a clear plastic bag holding Carter's black and yellow shoes. Seeing them, Lena felt her throat constrict. He was alive but in terrible danger, and she couldn't get anyone to believe it. They thought they already knew his fate; she could see it in the young security officer's compassionate expression.

Surely his parents would push for answers, grasp at the hope that he could be found.

Once the security officer left, other passengers, people who had met the Masseks during the previous week, filed through the room, offering support and comfort to the parents. Lena didn't see Kellie Rose Roberts among them, and wondered about that as she joined the end of the procession.

Only one or two others remained with Jay and Janelle when Lena's turn came. She held out her hand to grasp Janelle's. "Please...," she started saying.

Ignoring the hand, Janelle said curtly, "Thank you for coming, Miss Albright. Goodbye."

Lena wasn't expecting to be summarily dismissed so she hurried her speech. "Please. We need to talk. I think I know..."

Interrupting again, Janelle asked pointedly, "Do you have children?"

The question had always made Lena uncomfortable. She shook her head.

"Then you have no idea what we're going through," she snapped.

Coming from Janelle, the idea that parenthood instilled a superior empathy aggravated Lena, but she kept calm as she asserted, "I think your child is still alive. We have to continue the search."

Carter's mother caught her breath. "That's cruel," she said, lip starting to quiver. "Pushing false hope on grieving families."

"I'm serious. She wouldn't have committed suicide, not last night. She was excited about turning twelve. She was excited about Stockholm. Surely you know that. I tried to explain to Detective Vanin but..."

"How dare you suggest you know my daughter better than I do," Janelle fired back.

"What do you want?" Jay Massek broke in rudely. "Is it money? Do you think you're a psychic or something?"

"Nothing. I don't want anything. But people who commit suicide aren't making plans. When we said goodbye yesterday evening, she wasn't depressed. I think something else happened to her."

"I have no idea what you're talking about," Janelle said. "Are you saying she ran away?"

Lena tried to explain. "Carter made a comment once about being stalked. I thought it was a kid's imagination. But now.... Do you know anyone who was trying to get close to him?" She hoped they would come up with Kellie Rose's name on their own. It would make her task easier.

"Jennifer," Jay insisted. "That's her name. Jennifer."

"Yes, I'm sorry. Jennifer. Maybe someone you know...."

Janelle's face twisted in outrage. "No one we know would harm our little girl!"

So much for being subtle, Lena thought. "How about Kellie Rose Roberts? Your... daughter believed that..."

"That's blatant bullshit," Carter's father said. Visibly agitated, he stormed from the room, slammed shut the bedroom door.

Janelle stayed behind, but not with a friendly expression. "Our daughter believed all sorts of nonsense," she said tersely.

"She was afraid of Mrs. Roberts. Did you know that?" Lena realized she was exaggerating Carter's reaction, but she had to get taken seriously somehow.

Janelle took a step back; she clearly did not know this. Regaining her composure, she shook her head emphatically. "Well, I can promise you that Kellie Rose was as good as gold to our daughter. If you knew her at all, you'd know what a wonderful person she is."

"Her friendship could have been a ploy, so she could kidnap your child."

"Kellie Rose kidnap her?!" Janelle paused in shock. "What would be the point? Of all people, Kellie

Rose knows we can't pay a ransom. We have no money to pay anything."

Lena's eyes inadvertently roamed over the fine touches in the upscale stateroom.

Janelle reacted defensively. "This is a show, all right? As if it's any of your business or that detective friend of yours. We're looking for investors. My husband's business is in difficult straits right now. We thought gambling would work out. My husband has a system. But we're only breaking even. Then we met Kellie Rose and, just in passing, she said she was looking for investment opportunities. Last night, Jay laid out a business proposal and she said it was perfect. She's investing half a million in our business, more to come if things work out. We were supposed to sign the papers today, but it's been postponed. She certainly wouldn't kidnap our little girl."

Meanwhile, Jay Massek had returned to the room and stood next to his wife, one arm possessively across her shoulders. "And what about you?" he asked Lena. "You seemed awfully interested in our child. It's not normal that a grown woman would hang around with an eleven-year old. What were you doing with our daughter?"

Beneath the comment, Lena heard the implication of pedophilia. Profoundly offended, she exploded, "That eleven-year-old sought me out. And you know what? I didn't mind, because your child is smart and thoughtful and... and... deeply lonely." To hell with civility, she thought. "His own parents couldn't be bothered with him, so he turned to a stranger. But it's not me you should be worried about. This is a whole boatload of strangers. You're a gambler, Mr. Massek. What are the odds that all four thousand of them are fine upstanding citizens? That not one of them would consider hurting your child? What are the odds of that?!"

"Get out!" Janelle screamed.

But Lena was already out the door.

And instantly regretted her intemperate remarks. There was no way now the parents would approach Ship Security and insist they search Kellie Rose Roberts' stateroom. Lena had to find another way.

18

Lena's morning was spent searching for Kellie Rose in every place she could imagine. She tried the spa, the shops, the cafés. For a while, she hung around the outside door to the Sanctuary, in case Kellie Rose dropped in on the Masseks again. If she could spot the woman, she could track her back to her stateroom, Lena reasoned. When she left again, Lena could sneak in and free Carter. She wasn't yet clear in her mind how she would do that, but she thought she could persuade the room steward to help. She just had to find the right corridor and the right words.

Noon came without any trace of Kellie Rose Roberts. Dispirited, Lena realized she might never find the woman this way. The ship was too large and her prey too devious. With increasing desperation, Lena decided to appeal to the staff at Passenger Service. If she could convince them she was a friend, they might tell her Kellie Rose's room number.

She was on her way there when a voice stopped her mid-stride. People were talking about the missing child. Lena stealthily moved closer to eavesdrop. Peering around a corner into a laundry room, she saw two stewards conversing as they folded towels.

"Oh, God, I am so relieved. I mean, it's sad that kid drowned, but at least it's not a murder or kidnapping. Can you imagine how awful that would be?"

"I'm just happy the search has been called off. It's been impossible to work all morning with security poking around..."

Had Carter drowned after all? The news struck her like a physical blow.

In a numb trance, she stumbled to her room to call Marcus. He didn't answer. Guessing where he and his father were having lunch, she quickly made her way to the Charthouse dining hall.

Rushing off the elevator, she almost collided with Marcus' father.

"Oh! Sorry, Pavel." she said, pulling up in time.

"Who are you?" he said in alarm. "How do you know my name?!"

He had forgotten their meeting yesterday, she realized. "Remember me? I'm Lena. I have to talk with your son."

"Did you say KGB?"

Before she could respond, Marcus caught up with them. "She's okay, Pop. She's undercover. She's working with us."

"I see." Pavel nodded knowingly at her. "You're with the president, too."

Marcus sighed and held the elevator door open for his father. "Hello again, Lena." His tone was friendly but solemn.

The elderly man signaled to her as he boarded the elevator. "It's not safe out there. Get inside," he said urgently.

Lena slipped in behind Pavel. In a low frantic voice, she whispered to the detective, "Carter drowned?"

Marcus looked at her sadly. "The investigation's just been wrapped up. I was going to call you once my father was napping."

"You found his body then." She could barely say the words.

"No, the body hasn't been found. The search in the Gulf of Finland continues but...." He left the obvious unsaid, that too many hours had passed for the child to have survived in forty-degree waters.

She was, for the moment, speechless with relief. Misreading her silence, Marcus softly added, "I'm truly sorry. He was a remarkable kid."

She waved off the condolence. There was no body; his death wasn't confirmed. "I heard they called off the search."

"The search of the ship. After a full investigation, Chief Bronson's determined the child went overboard."

"He couldn't have!" Lena insisted. "You can't give up on Carter yet. Please."

Marcus paused and rubbed the back of his neck. He hadn't expected an argument. "This isn't a casual determination. Chief Bronson and his staff have experience with this sort of tragedy. People go miss-ing on cruise ships more often than most of us real-ize."

"Carter's missing, but that doesn't mean he..."

"The child is not on board," he said simply. "There's no evidence whatsoever of any crime. Every-thing points to suicide, including the heated argu-ment he had with his parents about six o'clock last night, right before you saw him. Which, by the way, you didn't mention this morning."

"It wasn't relevant," she interjected. "Kids fight all the time with their parents."

"It's very relevant, and you know it. And we found his phone. It was in the jumble of blankets that Mrs. Massek moved off the sofa. It looks like Carter recorded a suicide note before he went to the gym to get the weights."

She took a step back. A suicide note? She felt her gut twist.

Marcus solemnly added. "It was recorded last night at nine twenty-seven. Security will access it when we get to Stockholm tomorrow. The ship doesn't have the equipment to break his password, and we don't have enough time here at port to do it in Hel-sinki. But Chief Bronson is sure it's the note we've been looking for."

All Lena could do was stare at him as she pro-cessed the information. "They haven't heard it yet." A sliver of hope.

"No, but they will. His parents could open the phone itself but not the note. Carter added another layer of security...."

Frowning in thought, Lena interrupted, "Why would he do that, if it's a suicide note?"

That moment, Pavel grabbed his son's arm. "I have to go now, Marcus. I need to use the toilet."

Instantly, the filial side of Marcus surfaced. "Try to hang on, Pop. We're almost there."

"Aren't suicide notes usually left in noticeable places?" Lena pressed. "Isn't that the whole point of a suicide note, that it's read?"

Before she finished, though, the elevator doors opened and the two men rushed out. Marcus had his father's, briskly guiding him to the correct corridor. Lena stayed an anxious half step behind them. Almost at the end of the hallway, Marcus unlocked their door and stood aside as his father pushed into the bathroom. Only then did he turn to face Lena.

"Maybe Carter wasn't leaving the note for his parents. Maybe he was leaving it for someone else." Standing halfway in the doorway, he leaned toward her. "Do you know what password he might have chosen?"

His implication was clear, that Carter might have written the note for her. Shocked, Lena stared down at the blue and green swirls on the ship's carpet, a chill coursing down her back. She had an idea of what password he might have used, but she didn't want to say it. She didn't want the note revealed. She didn't want their suspicions confirmed.

"Lena?" Marcus asked, looking meaningfully at her.

She ached when she looked up at him. Finally, she said, "Try Tobias. Or Animorphs."

He pulled a notebook from his pocket. "Could you spell them for me?"

In a daze, she did. Then she shook her head, hope slowly returning. "That doesn't mean it's a suicide note. Earlier in the evening, I had told him about keeping a journal and he said he would do it on his phone. An audio recording." Her voice grew more confident. "An encrypted suicide note doesn't make sense. He would have wanted his parents to read it, not me. He would have wanted to explain himself or lash out or apologize. That's what suicide notes do. However," she paused for emphasis, "he *wouldn't* have wanted them to read his private journal."

Marcus stepped back into the corridor, closing the door behind him. "The case is closed. Let it rest, Lena."

"No, it is not closed. Not to me." She struggled to find traction on a convincing argument. "You'll see. You'll read the note and you'll see it's not a suicide."

"At this point, the note is *pro forma*. Security has already made the official determination..."

"But my fliers are gone," she exclaimed. "Isn't that suspicious? The kidnapper must have..."

"Security took them down. They've been inundated all morning with calls from terrified passengers." He rubbed his eyes. "You've got to understand. We're like a small town, full of strangers, with no escape. One false rumor sends people into a panic."

"It's not a false rumor," she countered. She sensed he was getting ready to go, so she swiftly added, "And what about Kellie Rose? Did they search her room?"

"I'm not at liberty to discuss the case with you." His tone was brusque, friendliness gone.

Lena gritted her teeth. She wasn't deterred; she was used to social opprobrium. "Then it hasn't been searched," she snapped.

"I didn't say that. But since you're being persistent, let me be blunt. She is no longer a person of interest. Take that as you will. The case is closed," he repeated slowly and firmly.

"But..."

Ignoring her, he opened the room door. Before he entered, though, he paused in thought. "Lena, I have to ask you something," he said.

She blinked, taken aback. "Okay."

"The goth culture - I guess the term is - seems to focus on death and suffering. Like Poe's famous poem, *The Raven*. Was Carter drawn to it? Did you talk to him about being a goth? His parents think you might have influenced ..."

She stepped back, instantly outraged. "What? Recruited Carter into a Satanic cult?! And that's why he killed himself?! Well, screw them."

Unperturbed by her outburst, Marcus tried to sound conciliatory. "You might have said something - inadvertently - that romanticized death."

She was having none of it. "Goth culture, as you call it, is not about death. It's about honesty. About rejecting the elaborate lies people construct around themselves. In fact, it's the opposite of this ship," and her arm swept around dramatically. "This is all bull-shit illusion. The chandeliers, the drinks, the fun and games, all to convince ourselves we're perfect and im-mortal and death can't touch us. That's what we're paying for. The illusion. And that's what I reject. But did I tell that to Carter? No. I'm not an asshole."

"That's what I thought. Thanks for the password. I'll ..."

But Lena stomped away before he could finish. Her heart was racing, her breath ragged. That was it, she fumed. She was washing her hands of the official inquiry. She'd open her own investigation. She'd find the truth. By herself.

19

Lena strode up the stairs to her stateroom; better to burn off her fury; easier to avoid people. And she especially wanted to avoid people. They aggravated her too much, their smugness, pettiness, idiocy.

Once in her room, she dropped onto the desk chair and found her journal. First order of business, constructing a time line of Carter's whereabouts the previous evening. Turning to an empty page, she scrawled "Time line" at the top. Her hand was shaking; her writing was terrible. She sat quietly for a moment to calm her breathing. Then, raising her pen again, she recounted everything Carter's parents and the police had said about last night, and added everything she remembered as well, noting the source of the information in parentheses.

6:15 – 7:25 p.m. I talk with Carter; he leaves for dinner with parents (me)
7:30 – 9 p.m. Dinner at Chez Pierre: Jay, Janelle, Kellie Rose & Carter (Jay's testimony but verifiable)
9:05 p.m. Carter & Janelle return to suite & Janelle leaves him (Janelle & Jay's testimony)

9 - 11 p.m. Business discussion between Jay & Kellie Rose, Janelle joining (Jay's testimony)
9:27 p.m. Carter makes audio recording (evidence)
9:40 p.m. Carter goes to gym (key card)
After 9:40 p.m. Carter leaves jacket at gym (evidence)
11 p.m. Carter's parents return to suite (Jay's testimony)
Est. 12:20 - 1:15 a.m. Carter not topside (me)
3 a.m. Brief but heavy rainstorm
5 a.m. Carter's trainers found, damp from rain (evidence)

There was something she was forgetting, Lena frowned. Probably trivial, but every little bit could help. What was it? Then she remembered and added to the list:

Approx. 1 a.m. Man with shopping bag on deck 15, walking toward steps to deck 16 (me).

Did he ascend? She didn't notice at the time. He might have stayed on deck fifteen to drink his beer. She wondered if he had seen something.

She studied the timeline. Between nine-thirty and nine-thirty-five, Carter had left his stateroom. Lena assumed he left voluntarily; there was no sign of forced entry, and Kellie Rose Roberts was with the parents the whole time. By nine-forty, he was at the gym, according to his key card. Someone else could have used it, of course, although that seemed unlikely. After all, his jacket was there. Too bad the CCTV cameras there were faulty.

Did that mean he was kidnapped at the gym? Lena checked its location on the map in her room. The Sea Dreamers Fitness Center was on deck fourteen forward. The exclusive Sanctuary area was on deck fourteen aft. Carter might have simply forgotten the jacket; he wouldn't have needed it to return to his suite from the gym.

But he didn't return, so where did he go? What did the ship cameras show? If only she could get into the security office.

Lena decided to visit the gym instead. She still had a few leftover fliers; she could post some of them there.

When she pushed through the gym's glass door a few minutes later, she saw only one person. It was a man about her age, wearing shorts and tee-shirt, working out on an elliptical machine. Its whirling sound was masked by upbeat rock music designed to get the body moving and heart pumping. Its pounding rhythms heightened Lena's anxiety.

The man on the elliptical heard nothing outside his head; he was wearing earbuds. Lena made a mental note to see if Carter had headphones or earbuds.

Maybe that was important; he wouldn't have heard someone sneaking up on him.

At that moment, the man looked up, saw her and almost fell off the machine. He glared at her as he righted himself.

Lena winced. She was sorry she had startled him. Further, with her customary black clothes and boots, she clearly didn't belong.

The man continued his workout for a few more minutes while she left fliers on the weight benches. Then he stopped, checked his pulse, wiped his forehead with one of the ship's white towels, and headed toward the door.

"Wait a second," Lena said, digging a flier from the stack she still clutched. "Have you seen this kid around? He comes to the gym."

The man gave it a cursory glance, then shook his head. "Have a good workout," he smirked as he pushed through the glass gym door.

"Thanks," she said. Lena automatically said thanks, even when people were being sarcastic.

Now she had the place to herself. She didn't know what she was hoping to find. Something hinting at Carter's last minutes there? She didn't even know where - precisely - his jacket had been found. She recalled the missing ten-pound weights and checked out the weight rack. Eight and twelve-pound barbells were present, but there was a gap where the tens should have been. Whoever took them hadn't returned them. Her own theory was that Kellie Rose had tossed them overboard when she positioned his shoes near the fake suicide point. That would have been after eleven, because she was with the Masseks until then. So where was Carter before eleven?

Lena sat on the weight bench and thought. Maybe someone else was involved, someone who grabbed Carter while Kellie Rose was establishing her alibi. Sure, it complicated the plan, but that had to be it. A mystery accomplice.

She tried to recall if anyone else had seemed overly interested in Carter. Maybe the balding man who sat with Kellie Rose at breakfast yesterday, the one with the coffee. He could have been covertly checking Carter out. That would make sense; he wouldn't want to nab the wrong child. Lena could feel excitement mounting as she considered it. Kellie Rose had only pretended not to know him. Maybe she and the man had planned to kidnap Carter in St. Petersburg. When that failed, they would have shifted to Helsinki. It made sense! What did the man look like? Lena searched her memory: portly, perhaps in his sixties, a moustache, no beard. Yesterday, he had been wearing what? A blue button-down shirt and slacks. So, he dressed more formally than many passengers, a way to instill trust, just like Roberts did.

Abruptly Lena stood up, her optimism soaring. She knew she could find him; she just had to start looking!

And just as suddenly, it crashed. "What am I doing?" she groaned, dropping back to the weight bench, her head falling into her hands. The man was just a man, no one special. She was grasping at straws, she realized miserably, and Marcus was right. For all of her preaching about rejecting illusion, she was a master at it. Telling herself lies, constructing a tantalizing fantasy that Carter was still alive.

Lena sobbed. Maybe she was crazy.

20

Irritation was Aurora's first reaction to the news. Why the hell did the kid have to go and kill herself? Aurora almost let the aggravation slip into her voice when Jay had called this morning with the news. Janelle was too upset to speak, he said.

At the time, Aurora had been putting on the finishing touches of her disguise. She'd had to pause and gather her wits before she could serve up the soothing platitudes they expected to hear. When she hung up, though, she hurled the bottle of rosy peach makeup across the stateroom. It clattered against the far wall but didn't break.

What a monumental waste of time, she fumed. Her plan had been so perfect. Now, the cruise was mere days from ending, and Aurora had no more prospects on the line. Management would not be happy.

Failure happened occasionally, as it did last February when her cruise turned out to be comprised solely of geriatrics. She had talked Management into backing that venture, because surely there would be grandchildren among them, easily lured away from elderly passengers who took long naps in the afternoons and didn't see or hear too well. But there were only two kids on board and both too young. From

Aurora's point of view, ten was the cut-off age. She had been ten when she had her first sexual experience, and it hadn't hurt her. But not younger than that. After all, she wasn't a monster.

Management had given her a pass on that one. But this time? She'd been so close to success. On top of that, this kid was astonishingly attractive; even Management had been excited when she'd sent photos. No, they wouldn't be happy at all.

She had to see if there were any other prospects. The operation wouldn't go as smoothly as she had expected of this one. No time to cultivate another set of parents. Good thing Eddie was around and had the giant aluminum suitcase with its discretely drilled air holes. They'd have to do an old-fashioned grab and drag tonight if they wanted to offload the cargo in Stockholm early tomorrow as planned.

First, though, she had to visit the Masseks, listen to Janelle wail, share a stiff drink with Jay. If they asked about investment plans, she'd reassure them. She didn't want them telling other people she was heartless; she still had an image to maintain for a few more hours.

Aurora sighed, straightened the collar of her black silk shirt and made her way to their stateroom.

After scanning the lunch crowd in the Galley Buffet and Charthouse, Aurora finally found Eddie Boltman in the Irish pub, knocking back a mug of something dark and foamy. Damn Eddie; he'd broken Rule One: no drinking. She suppressed a fierce urge to slap him, knowing she didn't want him pissed off. She'd need his cooperation after all. Which galled her, but that was how things were. For the moment, anyway.

When he saw her approaching his bar stool - the only one occupied in the shamrock wall-papered space - he'd smiled like the cat that ate a canary; she could almost visualize a bird's claw protruding from his fat mouth. He said nothing as she perched next to him. They were alone; the bartender was in a walk-in closet behind the bar, rummaging among boxes of standard beers and exotic micro-brews.

She lowered her voice. "You probably haven't heard, but the operation's off. The kid jumped last night."

Eddie took a giant swig and wiped his mouth with the back of his hand. "You don't say."

Strange; she was expecting him to be as upset as she was. As far as he knew, it was his paycheck, too. "We have to see if there are any other prospects on board. We don't have much time," she added, looking pointedly at the half-full mug.

He shrugged and downed more beer.

Eddie knew something, she realized. He was too nonchalant. He knew something about the kid. When the bartender returned and asked Aurora what she'd like to drink, she waved him off, stood and signaled for Eddie to follow her out. He didn't budge. "We have to talk," she said with a false amiability. "Figure this out together. Someplace quiet."

He paused a moment, swallowed his remaining beer, and turned to the bartender. "I'll be right back," he said.

He followed her to the elevator. They rode up in silence until they reached deck fifteen, passed through the crowded Galley Buffet and exited out of its glass doors into a cold brisk wind. Eddie now took the lead to the unoccupied glass smoking enclosure.

Aurora figured they were still in sight of a CCTV camera, but she knew it didn't record sound. She dug a cigarette from her pocket and lit up, as if this was the whole point of being there. As she exhaled a gray cloud, she stared off the port side toward Helsinki. Not as many people were disembarking today; the news of the suicide must be putting a damper on the high spirits of Sea Dream Cruisers.

Eddie positioned himself next to her, arms crossed over his muscled chest, also staring out.

She glared sidelong at him. "You have the kid, don't you?" He didn't answer so she said sharply, "You grabbed her last night."

He grunted. "You didn't tell me the kid's a girl."

"I pointed her out to you. Couldn't you tell?"

"How the hell was I supposed to tell? Talks like a boy, dresses like a boy…"

Her suspicions were confirmed; he had acted on his own, cutting her out of the loop, and it infuriated her. "What the hell difference does it make? We had a plan and you screwed it up."

"I screwed nothing up, you stupid bitch," he snarled. "And it makes all the difference. I was feeling sorry for the little guy, helping him work out with weights, encouraging him. I almost called off the operation, just let the poor skinny kid alone. Then, when I was spotting him with free weights last night, I noticed something. The kid was laying flat on the weight bench holding up a twenty-pound bar, and I notice there wasn't a bulge where there should be a budge. Not even a tiny little pecker. So, I ask, nice and friendly, 'Say, are you fooling me? Are you a girl?' When she don't answer, I say, 'Show me you're not a girl.' And she still says nothing and that's when I know."

His expression dark, Aurora wondered in horror if he took the kid and pitched her over the railing. He certainly looked capable of it.

Eddie continued. "I get the water bottle, already set up, and tell her she's got to stay hydrated. When I give it to her, I tell her it'll taste funny because there's protein powder in it. And she drinks the whole goddamn bottle, just like that."

"You idiot," is all that Aurora can think to say. "It's all recorded on CCTV."

"No, it ain't. I took care of the cameras earlier."

She didn't relent. "You have her stashed where? In your room? How long before she wakes up and starts screaming? How long do you think you can keep the room steward from checking?"

"I got that all figured out, too. Don't you worry. Her mouth is taped shut and I got plenty of the drug. And I have that little 'Don't disturb' light above the door so the steward stays clear. I know what I'm do-ing."

She railed on, "And now Ship Security is all over the disembarkation area. You'll never get her off."

"Sure I will," he angrily countered. "Not today. I was going to, but those goddamned fliers are all over and every woman on board is giving me the stink eye. All I need is some hysterical bitch demanding I open my case."

"You're running out of time and ports," Aurora observed coldly.

"Tomorrow morning it'll be different. People are here for a fun vacation. They don't want to spend too much time thinking about sad or scary shit. They want to think it's a suicide. Clean and simple; can't happen to them or their kids. And the crew's already taking down those fucking fliers."

"In Stockholm, I could have waltzed right off this ship with her and no questions asked. Her parents agreed that...."

"Crazy bitch, the kid hates you. I seen you talking to him at breakfast yesterday. He - I mean, she – would never go with you. She'd never drink anything you gave her either, so don't fool yourself you could have drugged her. She trusted me, not you." He put his fists on his hips. "Ha! That's a nice turnabout for a change."

Aurora wheeled on him, fury reddening her face. "You piece of shit, I...."

"No, you listen. The kid was never going to go with you, saw right through your phony ass. You failed, Aurora or whoever the hell you are. You failed, and I didn't. What do you think Management will say to that?" He read something menacing in her expression then, so he added, "And you tell a fucking soul about this, I'll dump the kid overboard and go straight to Ship Security to report you. How you tried to get me involved in kidnapping, but how I refused. I was the kid's friend; that's what the cameras will show." He stepped closer and Aurora involuntarily moved back. "Even if they think I'm in on it, they'll never think I'm the brains behind it. That's you, Aurora. You and Management. I go down, you all go down with me."

He straightened, adjusted his elastic waist nylon pants, and strode back inside.

Aurora didn't immediately follow. With a last, deep drag on her cigarette, she controlled her anger and considered her options. Not ideal, but she could salvage the operation. She'd disembark first in Stockholm and get Eddie and the suitcase into the right taxi. He'd have to take it. What choice did he have, hop on a bus? Then everything would go as planned.

She stubbed out the butt. Seven minutes after Eddie's departure, face set in grim determination, Aurora returned inside.

Lena, who had watched the drama unfold, didn't see that part. She was already on Eddie's tail.

21

Lena saw the encounter by happenstance, because she'd decided to repost the fliers in the video arcade on deck fifteen. Desolate, she had just been going through the motions, trying to come to terms with the fact that Marcus was probably right.

But as she left the warm interior of the Galley Buffet, she saw something that stopped her. Kellie Rose Roberts and a large man together in the glass smoking enclosure. He seemed faintly familiar, but she could have seen him anywhere in the past six days of cruising.

She stepped closer and then ducked into the shadows to watch. They were looking away from her and their words were indistinct, but their body language was clear: the woman was furious and imperious, a captain who has been disobeyed. The man's posture was stubbornly belligerent, a resentful and unreliable subordinate.

The accomplice! Lena clapped a hand against her mouth to silence her gasp: she was right after all. It made so much sense. This guy clearly worked out. He could have found Carter in the gym and easily hauled him away. That gave him access to the missing weights, too. Another realization dawned: it looked like the same man with the shopping bag who had passed her the night before. Lena imagined him carrying the weights and Carter's shoes to the fake suicide point.

When the man stormed off, she knew there was no time to get Marcus. She quickly followed; she had to get his name or room number.

Lena made herself stay close enough to touch him. His back was broad, tee-shirt too small. He could snap her neck in half, she realized. Scaredy Cat Maggie, she reproached herself, pulse racing in fear and fury. Once he was halfway through the Galley Buffet, though, keeping up with him was more difficult. Other passengers pushed between them, slowing her down. Her height helped; she could see over the heads of most of the passengers. If only she could get past this large family.

An enormous crash startled her, and she involuntarily whipped around to its source: one of the tray carts had upended, sending glasses, plates and silverware clattering. The distraction took only seconds, but it was enough. When she turned back to her quarry, he was gone.

But she now had a name. In the fleeting second before her eyes turned to the crash, she saw his face. Eddie, the giant man from the Atrium Bar all those nights ago.

☸

"I know who has Carter!" Marcus heard Lena's shout before he saw her.

He jerked his head around. "You found him?!" He leapt up from his seat in the ship's open-sided movie arena. He had been watching *Dirty Dancing* with his father and a scattering of other passengers. His father was humming along.

"No, but I know who must have him." Lena was next to him now, unable to keep her voice down despite the shushing sounds from other movie patrons.

His heart sank. This sounded like more of the same from Lena, he thought. He wondered if she was the type he'd encountered a few other times in his career: the well-meaning busybody who loves being the center of attention. Not that he didn't like her, but she was starting to wear on him.

"Kellie Roberts again?" Marcus asked with resignation.

"No, no." Lena said impatiently. "Her accomplice!"

Of course there would be an accomplice, Marcus sighed. "And how do you know this?"

"They were arguing thirty or forty minutes ago. On the top deck, away from everybody else."

"And you overheard them?"

"Well, no. But I could tell they were arguing," Lena insisted. "I'm sure it's the same man I saw carrying a plastic bag on the roof the night Carter disappeared. And..."

Marcus could tell she wouldn't stop talking until he heard her out, so he held up his hand and led her several paces away from his father and the rest of the audience.

Once they were away from the others, he tersely observed, "You didn't mention a man on the roof before."

"No, I forgot about him until now. And, listen to this, the guy obviously works out. I'll bet he was at the gym last night with Carter. You can check the key cards and security cameras to confirm it."

"I told you already, the cameras in that area are on the fritz. And, in terms of the key cards to access the gym, that's already been checked. Until an early riser got there at four-thirty this morning, Carter's is the only one recorded. He was alone in the gym last night."

"He couldn't have been! That guy probably slipped into the gym behind him. Or he was there before eight and waiting. That's where he grabbed Carter, all while Kellie Rose was building her alibi." Lena saw the skepticism in Marcus' face, so she didn't repeat her earlier speculation about the sex trade. But to her way of thinking, Eddie's presence confirmed it.

"Kellie Roberts has been cleared," he told Lena again, but even so dug a notepad and pen from his shirt pocket. "But, okay, I'll ask security staff to check him out. Did you happen to catch his name?"

"It's Eddie something. I don't know his last name."

"That's all you overheard?"

Uncomfortable, Lena shuffled her feet. "Well, he tried to pick me up a few nights ago. That's how I know it's Eddie."

Marcus put down the pen and looked at her. "It seems like quite a coincidence for your suspected accomplice to be the same man who tried to pick you up."

Lena didn't reply. His insinuation was humiliating, that she was making a wild accusation about a man because he had made a play for her. Marcus probably thought this was a ploy to make him jealous.

Sensing he had upset her, Marcus softened his tone. "Okay, we have a man who tries to pick up pretty women. Maybe he tried that with Kellie Roberts, too, and that's why she was chewing him out. Isn't that plausible?"

Lena stood her ground. "No. It wasn't that type of argument. I could tell from their body language."

Marcus wearily studied her for a moment. "Fine. His room number then?"

"I don't have that either. I was following him just now, but I lost him. I'd recognize him in a heartbeat if I could go through all of the passenger key card photos."

"Not possible. Company privacy policy."

"Or Ship Security can check the cameras near the deck fifteen smoking area for about one this afternoon. I'll bet they can run facial recognition software to link his photo to his key card's information."

"They aren't going to do that, Lena. That takes time and they're busy. Plus, the case is closed."

"This is important, Marcus. This is Carter's life. So what if they're shorthanded screening shopping bags and they miss a bottle or two of contraband wine?"

Her dismissive tone rankled him. "Just this morning, in addition to scouring the ship for any sign of Carter or foul play, they've had to respond to a domestic dispute and credit card fraud. They checked out almost two thousand passengers and hundreds of staff and crew. Now they're checking them back in, including every bag and purse and backpack. Looking not just for contraband wine, as you say, but guns, explosives, toxins, anything that could pose a threat to the health and safety of people on board. They do a terrific job, too."

She held up her palm to deflect his words. "All right, I get it. They're busy. I apologize." Lena was breathing heavily now, anxiety escalating as she realized that she was failing to convince Marcus.

Before she could launch into her tirade again, he interjected. "You look exhausted, Lena. Go back to your room and try to rest. This whole thing has understandably upset you. Losing Carter, blaming yourself." He took her arm and gently pivoted her toward the exit. "Go on and get some sleep. You need it."

The rest of the day was awful for Lena. She kept replaying the conversation with Marcus, wondering what she could have said to persuade him. She knew Eddie was the kidnapper, she knew she could identify him from a line-up. But Marcus wasn't interested. As far as he and Chief Bronson were concerned, Carter was a suicide. A statistic.

She had to do this alone, trusting her instincts, being brave. She couldn't waste time sleeping.

Instead of going to bed, she wandered, pale and silent, through the ship. Searching for either Kellie Rose or Eddie. Finding neither.

Mid-afternoon, she caught sight of herself in the massive mirror near the ice bar. Even to herself, she looked like the specter of a drowned woman, disturbing the living who just wanted to relax and play. After this, she avoided mirrors.

Lena agonized that Carter might already have been spirited off the ship and was now somewhere in Helsinki. Briefly, she debated with herself about searching the city before she concluded it was a ridiculous idea.

About five in the afternoon, as the ship was leaving port, she passed the Captain's Tea Room, an intimate café advertising teas from around the world. Sitting at a cozy corner table was Kellie Rose Roberts, knee-to-knee with a slumped and despondent Janelle. Lena steadied herself against the corridor wall as she realized what this meant. Carter was still on the ship; Roberts wouldn't stay on board otherwise, she was sure.

Lena considered approaching the two women and publicly accusing Kellie Rose of stealing the child, but thought better of it. That would only put Roberts on high alert. Better if she just watched and waited from a distance, hiding behind a display of art on sale. Poetic justice, Lena thought grimly, she's become the stalker of Carter's stalker.

Soon after six, the two women stood and wandered aft at a leisurely pace. Kellie Rose had her arm around Janelle's shoulders. Lena left her post and followed several feet back, trying to stay inconspicuous. When they came to the bank of elevators, Lena decided she would get on the elevator with them, rather than risk losing Kellie Rose. But before she got to it, a loud group of friends wearing equally loud Hawaiian shirts piled in. No space was left, even for skinny Lena.

Just as the doors were closing against her, she inadvertently made eye contact with her quarry. And Kellie Rose Roberts gave her the most chilling smile Lena had ever seen.

The rest of the evening's prowls produced nothing. Eventually, depressed and frightened for Carter, Lena stumbled to her stateroom, closed the drapes against the long twilight, and fell into a haunted sleep.

22

Troubling dreams of drowning, slimy seaweed wrapped around her legs, holding her under. She thrashed repeatedly, finally smashing her hand against the wall. That woke her with a jolt.

The bed sheet had pulled free and was twisted around her legs. Lena kicked it loose and sat up, still gulping for air. She felt momentarily confused about what she needed to do. It was something important. Then, with a rush of emotion, she remembered and fell back hard against the mattress. Carter.

The room clock glowed six thirty-two. She had to get up. She had to keep searching. But dizziness hit as soon as she stood. Light-headed from hunger, she hadn't eaten since the previous day's breakfast. She'd barely had anything to drink. If she was going to search, she had to get ready, and that meant getting something to eat. Quickly. She didn't want to waste time on food.

Lena splashed water on her face and combed her hair, but that was it. No time for makeup. No one here cared. She pulled on the same clothes she had worn yesterday, picking them up from the pile she'd left on the floor. She felt cold, even inside her stateroom, so she added the heavy black sweater.

Ten minutes later, she was in the Galley Buffet, wandering down the breakfast line, past the food station serving sausages and bagels, pancakes and eggs. Another offered piles of gorgeously colored fresh fruit. Nothing looked appetizing, but she grabbed a sugary cinnamon roll to eat as she walked. She could take it and a cup of tea with her as she continued her search of the ship.

The loudspeaker startled her as it sparked awake.

Good morning, Sea Dream Cruisers! It's another beautiful day on the Baltic. The Sea Dream has arrived at the port in Nynäshamn, Sweden. Everyone planning to take one of the fantastic shore excursions into Stockholm needs to check their tickets for their muster points. Tours will start at seven-thirty promptly! Those who are not taking a tour may begin disembarkation at seven on deck four forward. Remember: no sitting or standing on the stairways. Please be back on board by four o'clock. Happy sailing!

Nothing about bringing passports, she noted offhandedly. Not like Russia; passengers could easily come and go in Sweden.

Then a thunderbolt struck and she dropped the cinnamon roll. This was it, she instantly knew. This was where Eddie would leave the ship for good, smuggling Carter out with him. No one would think to stop him.

Eddie would want to be first in line, and that meant seven o'clock. Lena read the clock posted above the omelet station and her heart sank; it was already six forty-six. Deck four forward was eleven levels down and the length of the ship. She had to get there before Eddie did.

And she was running out of time.

23

Navigating briskly through the loitering breakfast diners and coffee servers, Lena passed the cheerful crew member proffering hand sanitizer and finally reached the corridor. Clear of the crowd, she broke into a run toward the deck fifteen aft bank of elevators. None was there, so she punched the DOWN button and paced impatiently. At that moment, several groups of diners emerged from the breakfast buffet and milled between her and the closed elevator doors. Foreseeing stops on every residential floor, Lena abandoned the elevator idea and dashed down the steps.

But after running down three flights, she had to stop for breath. She checked the time again and was shocked that so many minutes had passed. Conceding to herself that she was descending too slowly, she forced herself to wait for an elevator.

In an eternity, it finally arrived. Still full but not as packed as before; the riders jostled and politely made space for her.

Lena looked for the elevator button to deck four but there wasn't one, so she pushed the one for deck six, remembering that it ran the length of the ship. From the Estonia and St. Petersburg departures, she knew she could then take the stairs down two flights to deck four and the disembarkation area.

The elevator started to descend, then stopped on deck eleven. Again, on deck nine. A third time on deck eight. Each time, riders departed and new ones boarded. In agony, Lena realized she had stopped breathing. Finally, with only three other people left on the elevator, the doors opened on deck six. She rudely pushed past them, shouting an apology over her shoulder, and began to race toward the front of the ship.

Her eyes barely registered the shuttered shops and bars she passed, the paintings on display, the winding grand staircase up to the casino. Unconsciously, her steps fell into rhythm with a Latin song blasting from the ship's sound system.

As she ran, she imagined what she would find at the disembarkation area. Eddie would have stuffed Carter into a duffle bag or large box or suitcase. That's what she could look for. Then a spark of doubt: *What if Eddie was empty-handed? It was possible that Kellie Rose might be carrying Carter, but could she really? She didn't look especially strong.* Lena's uncertainty started to burn. *What if Carter wasn't unwilling and was leaving the ship on his own volition? Maybe he liked Eddie, mistaking him for a friend.*

Self-doubt blazed now: *Maybe he liked Eddie more than he liked her. And what if Eddie really was a friend? He could be rescuing Carter from Kellie Rose; that's what their argument could have been about.*

Lena's steps faltered, her thoughts in disarray. She wasn't sure she could rely on her instincts after all.

Then she remembered Carter's expression the last time she had seen him. She had read hope there, and trust. Their friendship mattered to him. She mattered.

Cursing her corrosive doubt, she doubled her pace, her long legs making up for the lost seconds. When she reached the staircase, she flew down, two steps at a time.

She would never ever betray that trust.

The disembarkation area was located on the port side, in a large room only a few steps from the elevator and a few more steps from the stairway. With a low white ceiling, florescent lights and gray-blue carpet, the area was utilitarian, unlike every other public space on the ship. The only items breaking the monotony of the stark white walls were a round clock and a poster reminding passengers of what not to bring on board.

The procedure was simple, as Lena remembered it: Exiting passengers formed two queues between red rope lines, each queue leading to a white podium with a built-in computer. As passengers reached the podium, they inserted their key cards into a slot in the front, and the computer went into action, pulling up their names, photographs and room numbers. Only after a crew member checked that data against each passenger was the key card returned and the person permitted to leave. Fast and efficient. Then outside, over the narrow gangway that spanned a meter of dark water, a passenger was on the pier and free to leave.

When Lena arrived, security personnel lined the walls. Hands clasped in front, legs slightly apart, they looked alert yet relaxed. This was a routine disembarkation. Later in the day, they'd be busier because then they would have to check every incoming bag. A luggage screener was set up for that purpose, but it wasn't in use now.

From the corridor, Lena peered into the disembarkation area. The clock showed six fifty-nine. She'd made it. Eddie wasn't even in line yet, she realized in relief, rubbing her mouth.

Then suddenly she grasped that people were moving; they already were being checked through. It was too early! Her eyes swept again over the two lines of passengers. Marcus and his father, she noticed, were leaving the podium on the left and heading to the gangway. Had Eddie already gotten through?

Lena couldn't believe she was too late; she refused to believe it. Instead, she paced the hallway in a circuit: stairs, elevator, disembarkation area, repeat. Fighting panic and exhaustion every step. She glanced into the disembarkation area again.

And there he was. Somehow, Eddie had materialized close to the front of the line on the right, rolling a mammoth aluminum-sided suitcase. She blinked. Had she been asleep on her feet?

"Stop!" she wanted to shout but then Eddie would run. She had to sneak in front of him, get to the gangway first. She could stop him there, demand he open his luggage.

Biting her lip against the urge to scream, she tried to slip between the rope lines. But a young security officer blocked her way and refused to let her pass. Signaling toward the line on the left, he told her she had to wait in line for clearance like everyone else.

Lena impatiently took her place. She surreptitiously studied Eddie to her right. His clearance was taking time, she noted, because he was permanently leaving the ship. Just as she arrived at the podium, she heard a crew member wish him safe travels. He was cleared.

Her anxiety roared as she waited for the return of her own card. Finally, the crew member handed it back and wished her a good day. She didn't even hear.

Blood pounding through her ears, she ran between the white podiums for the exit.

Eddie was several feet ahead of her, but his progress slowed as he maneuvered the heavy suitcase on to the gangway. The gangway wasn't long; in a few brisk steps, he would be on the pier.

Lena had no choice. In terror and fury, she launched herself at his back. Clutching on to his shoulders, she pummeled his head, shrieked at him to let Carter go.

Everyone was stunned, including Eddie. Lena - oblivious to Eddie's curses, to Marcus's shouts from the pier, to the sounds of security officers running at her - kept hitting and screaming and hitting.

Eddie twisted away from her and, for a brief instant, let go of the suitcase handle. Lena made a desperate lunge toward it. At that point, Eddie had reached the end of whatever marginal store of patience he had. With one powerful motion, he lifted her up and cast her off the side of the gangway.

Lena went flying into the air and over the safety netting. Her mind reeled. Vague impressions of clouds, the Sea Dream's vividly colored hull, a blue ship bumper attached to the pier.

Then she hit the greenish black water and quickly dropped down, down, down. Her mind splintered. One half unwittingly catalogued the experience: the coldness, the increasing darkness, the water flooding into her gaping mouth, the taste of diesel.

The other half thinking over and over: *I failed, I failed, I failed.*

Then her head struck something and blackness enveloped her.

24

Before she could open her eyes, Lena was aware of the pain. Deep behind her eyes, inside her skull, the length of her throat. The pain seared, so she drifted back to thoughtlessness and sleep.

The second time, while not ready for the pain, she was not so surprised by it, and wrestled with it to wake up. Someone was nearby; she sensed it. A possible threat; her body sought to push adrenaline into her system to coax her into awareness, but there wasn't enough. Or she didn't care. The pain won again, and she drifted back to thoughtlessness and sleep.

The third time, she felt herself push past the pain, and her eyelids flitted, finally cracked open. A shadow nearby. A shape. A man. Marcus.

He was standing at the window, staring out, cast in silhouette by filtered daylight. She didn't announce her consciousness, instead using the moment to observe. He was frowning in thought, intent and serious, the embodiment of a homicide detective. She marveled at her courage in standing up to him. And she had, repeatedly. Not that it mattered, she remembered with a deep stab of despair. She had lost in the end. Carter had lost in the end.

But then Marcus glanced toward her and a smile transformed his face.

"Lena, you're back," he said.

As if she had gone somewhere on holiday. Lena groaned at the absurdity of it.

He moved to her bedside. "How do you feel?"

She wanted to reply, readied her mouth to open, but no sound emerged. Only more pain and she whimpered.

He quickly added, "Never mind. You must feel like hell. Just rest. Don't try to talk." He made a move to take her hand but hesitated. "I'll talk for both of us."

She was now aware of where she was: a hospital room. She heard a beeping monitor near her head but was too stiff to turn to look at it. She wondered how long had she been here.

As if reading her mind, Marcus replied, "You're in a hospital in Stockholm. It's not quite four on Wednesday afternoon. You were out more than thirty-two hours, with the head injury. Plus, you nearly drowned, so they're monitoring you for possible pneumonia or respiratory distress. Can you sit up at all? I'll get more pillows."

With enormous effort, she groggily leaned an inch or two forward while he stuffed another pillow behind her head.

"There, now you can drink some water." He lifted a tall glass and inserted a paper straw between her dry lips, pallid without her bold red lipstick. "Try to drink a little," he urged.

She made an effort, she really did, but only a trickle coursed down her throat and it scorched. She fell back against the pillows.

"I've been very worried. Everyone's been. But you're awake now, that's the main thing. It's going to be all right." Her puzzled frown caused him to slowly repeat, "Everything is going to be all right because of you."

Her throat still burned. "Cart...?" She swallowed hard.

"Carter's fine, Lena. He's safe, here, in the hospital. He'd been tied up and heavily drugged but he's coming out of it. They dosed him with GHB." He added, "Gamma-hydroxybutyric acid. Sometimes used as a general anesthetic. You may have heard of it as a date rape drug."

She scrambled frantically to sit up.

"No, he's fine. No evidence of sexual assault. Here, lie back down." He smoothed her pillows, gently pushed her prone. Then he continued, "They used it to keep him quiet. Eddie Boltman stuffed him under his bed for a day and a half, so the kid had to be dosed a few times. They knew what they were doing. Carter only remembers being very thirsty, and drinking protein shakes or Dr. Pepper, which hid the drug's taste. There doesn't seem to be any permanent damage. He should be released in a few hours."

Carter was safe. Wave after wave of relief washed over her. He had made it. Lena's eyes burned with tears. She didn't notice this pain.

Pulling a chair next to the bed, he sat silently and waited. Eventually, he took her hand and softly squeezed. As his thumb caressed her palm, he said in a muffled voice. "I am so very sorry, Lena. We almost lost you both because I was an arrogant prick and didn't listen." He cleared the emotion from his throat. "Boltman and Roberts are child sex traffickers. They were hauling Carter off in Boltman's suitcase."

At this, Lena pulled her hand free, curled it under her chin, her hand mimicking the terrible image in her mind's eye, of Carter curled up in that aluminum box, about to be born into a world of rape and abuse. Property: used, sold, broken, abandoned. Devastated, she started to cry, unable to control herself. She wanted to forgive Marcus for doubting her, but she couldn't.

Marcus was quiet, almost crushed by remorse. He shook his head to clear it; after all, he was in the business of remorse. He couldn't let himself succumb to it. In a few minutes, he was able to speak again. "I listened to his recording. The one on his phone. You were right about that. He made no mention of suicide." Marcus leaned back. "But he talked a lot about you. You've made quite an impression on him. Now that he's feeling better, he's been asking to see you.

Once the doctor clears you for visitors, I'm sure he'll be here."

Her emotions upended, Lena now felt surging joy. "Carter here?" she whispered, hardly daring to believe it. Suddenly, panic struck; he could still be at risk. With an intense focus on Marcus's face, she urgently asked. "You got him...?"

He knew she meant Boltman. "Yes, he was caught immediately. Swedish authorities have him now." The assurance in his voice - his investigator voice - was returning. He was on solid ground here. "As I said, he'd hidden Carter under the bed, then kept on a Do Not Disturb light so the steward wouldn't go in to clean his room. He probably had to hold on to Carter longer than he expected. The ship's CCTV footage shows him lurking around the disembarkation point on Monday, but, for some reason, he decided against Helsinki. Maybe he thought everything would blow over by the time we got to Stockholm." Marcus brooded about Boltman, how close he had come to succeeding.

Lena broke in. "Kellie Rose...?" Her voice cracked.

"I'm not happy to tell you this. Roberts is still at large. That's not her name. Not even her real face." He grunted in frustration, then picked up the glass of water on Lena's bedside table and again held the straw to her mouth. She could swallow a little more this time. When she finished, he continued. "Of the two of them, I'm sure she was the one in charge, but Boltman could have acted without authorization. Other CCTV footage shows them arguing the day after Carter disappeared. You mentioned that, I remember."

Lena remembered it, too, and how Marcus had dismissed its importance. But she had missed vital clues as well. Why hadn't she listened to Carter's concerns? He had sensed the woman's dangerous masquerade from the start.

"The Masseks say Carter was supposed to go with Roberts to see the Vasa Ship Museum," Marcus explained. "They said they even spoke with the museum's associate director, getting his reassurance that Carter would be fine. But the real associate director is on holiday in Spain. They see now she planned to kidnap him that way."

Lena blinked, reassessing the blame she had apportioned to the Masseks. Roberts' plan was so elaborate that even conscientious parents could have been fooled.

Marcus turned to stare out of the hospital window again. "I think she could have gotten away with it. We're lucky, in a way, that Eddie got impatient. And incredibly lucky that you were there." He turned back to Lena.

"She's gone?" With the water, Lena's voice was marginally stronger.

"She was the first passenger off the ship, carrying only a handbag. No sign of her since. She didn't leave fingerprints in the room, or even hair in the shower drain. Or any luggage. I imagine she scrubbed the place and dropped her stuff overboard sometime in the night." He cleared his throat. "We think she and Boltman are part of a ring that preys on cruise ships. Other children have gone missing over the years. Looking at those reports, we may be able to see a pattern. Boltman's being interrogated now, but he doesn't seem to know much. Not even Roberts' real name. He calls her Aurora Borealis, but that doesn't match any of Interpol's records, so the search continues. At least we can alert cruise lines about the threat. And our guy Eddie's out of commission."

Lena nodded. The news of Robert's escape depressed her, and she wanted to shut it out. She closed her eyes.

But Marcus continued to talk. "The cruise line representatives will come by now that you're awake. You're a hero. They plan to offer you a cruise of your choice. That is, if you ever want to go on one again." He paused. "I should let you sleep. And I need to go anyway. My father's still on the ship. It's finally been cleared to leave."

Lena didn't respond, but she opened her eyes and watched him stand up, rub the back of his neck.

"I'm glad I was here when you woke up, to personally apologize and thank you. To tell you how much I admire you." He gave a rueful smile and added, "I don't think I've ever met anyone as tenacious or fierce as you are." Then he pulled out his wallet, extracted a business card and scribbled something on it. He placed the card on her bedside table, next to the glass of water. "I wouldn't blame you if you never wanted to hear from me again. But could you call me anyway, when you're home, to let me know you're okay? I'd appreciate it." He stood awkwardly for a moment.

She said nothing. Her feelings were jumbled but she didn't think she'd call. Too much water under the bridge.

"Who knows?" he added. "We might end up on the same cruise again someday. That would be interesting. We could solve crimes together on the high seas. Think about it."

Then he walked away from the bed. A nurse had approached and was standing in the doorway; she smiled broadly when she saw Lena.

"You're awake," she said brightly in accented English. "I'll let Dr. Karlsson know. He'll want to check on you himself." Then she noticed Marcus. "Hello, detective. How are you feeling?"

"Fine, I feel fine," he reassured her.

"Well, if that changes, see the ship's doctor right away. It's best to get completely checked out by your physician after you're home."

"I will," Marcus reassured her again. "Thanks." Then with a salute and half-smile at Lena, he left.

Lena's curiosity was piqued. "He's ill?"

The nurse made a distasteful face. "He swallowed some of that nasty port water. Not as much as you did, of course. We induced vomiting and put him on antibiotics, but we want to be safe." She studied the monitors, making notations in the medical chart.

"How did he swallow...?" Her voice gave out.

Briskly inspecting Lena's eyes and throat, the nurse replied, "He dove in to save you. Just in time, too. Didn't he tell you?"

Lena slept again and awoke feeling stronger, the pain subsiding, her head clearing. The room was quieter; no beeping noises. She was no longer hooked up to the monitor or attached to various tubes. She remembered Dr. Karlsson's checkup, but she wasn't sure if she had imagined the conversation with Marcus. Then she noticed his card and picked it up. He had scrawled on the back, "Please call."

He had saved her from drowning. He had saved her.

Studying his name on the card, she realized that there wasn't as much water under the bridge as she had thought. Maybe she would call.

25

Still light outside, Lena noted when she opened her eyes again. She vaguely wondered if it was the same day.

She could raise the glass of water by herself now. Then she carefully extricated herself from the bed-sheets and slowly walked to the toilet and back. When she returned to the room, she noticed her suit-case had been brought from the ship.

She was still very weak, but she managed to un-zip the bag and pull out a pair of black trousers. She slipped them on beneath the hospital gown. Suddenly aware that she felt cold, she found a long purple sweater and socks as well. Sufficiently dressed, she opened the door and peeked into the corridor.

"No, No! You shouldn't be up yet!" exclaimed a young nurse hurrying toward her.

"I need to see Carter Massek. Is he still here?"

"The boy in the suitcase? Yes, for a few more minutes. They'll check out soon, but he's been insist-ing on seeing see you. Stay here and I'll get him."

Reluctantly, Lena settled on the edge of the bed.

"Knock, knock," came a woman's voice she didn't recognize, American accent. "Can I come in?" It was Janelle Massek. "I heard you were awake."

"Of course," Lena said, although talking with Janelle was the last thing she felt like doing. She noticed that her voice was less rough than it had been. Her throat felt a little better also. "How's Carter?"

"She's doing okay. Poor darling, what an awful ordeal. She'll be here in a second, but I wanted to pop in first, to tell you how grateful I am - we both are - that you saved our baby." Here, Janelle's words failed. She had to pause a moment to breathe. "To think what might have happened..." They failed her again.

Lena wasn't inclined to help. Her sympathy was mixed with annoyance that Janelle continued to refer to Carter as a girl.

Sensing Lena's disapproval, Janelle bit her lip, looked uncertain. "I don't know what you must think of me, but I love my child very much. I'll support whatever she wants. It's just that...." She took a deep breath. "It's a shame she wants to be a boy. She's such a beauty."

Lena carefully but firmly shook her bandaged head. "Not wants. Is. It's not a choice. It's how he was born."

Janelle paused. "I suppose you're right. I just have to get used to the idea. The nurses here weren't shocked at all. One of them told me she has a brother who transitioned into a woman, if you can believe that." She gave a nervous smile, unsure what to think. Then she became solemn again. "It may take

us a little time, but we both want what's best for...."
She paused again and swallowed, "Carter. That's our
baby's name now. Carter."

Lena realized she had been holding her breath.
Now, exhaling, she said, "He needs that. Your love
and encouragement."

Janelle nodded. "I started to realize that when I
heard the recording he made. I'm really going to try.
And I'm sorry I misjudged you."

Lena could hear sounds from the hallway. People
approaching.

Janelle heard them too, and said in a rush, "Do
you think you can come out to see us sometime in
Lubbock? It would mean the world to Carter. To all of
us."

Surprised by the invitation, Lena felt touched
when she realized Janelle was asking quickly to protect Carter, in case she refused. But Lena wasn't
about to. "I'd love that. And your son can visit me anytime in Burbank." A little reluctantly, she added,
"You both, also. There's lots to see in the area." On
her own turf, she and Janelle might even find a way
to become friends. Well, not friends, exactly. Team-
mates.

"Lena!" Carter cried, suddenly rushing into the
room, climbing on the bed and tightly hugging her.

Jay was in his wake and awkwardly approached
Lena.

"We owe you our girl's life," he said. Janelle shot him a look and he corrected himself. "Our son's life. We can't thank you enough."

Janelle was on the job, Lena saw gratefully. In a little while, she'd tell them and Carter about puberty blockers. Someday soon, she would help them find resources and information about hormone injections and other treatment options. She would look out for Carter's interests, making sure that Jay and Janelle did not slide back to the old way of doing things. But not now; this moment was for celebrating.

She looked down at Carter's blond head, felt the strength of his arms encircling her and was overpowered with emotion. She closed her eyes and crooned, "You're safe now. You're safe." Eventually, she pulled back to look deeply into his light hazel eyes. "I'm coming to see you in Lubbock and you'll come to see me in Burbank. Your parents agree. Then, when you're eighteen, you can move to Burbank, if you like. You can find your community there."

She felt his shoulders start to shake beneath her arms, then noticed tears welling in his eyes, coursing down his perfect cheeks. "I love you, Lena," he whispered.

She wanted to cry, too, and laugh. "I love you, too, Carter," she declared, "with all my heart." And then - fiercely, protectively - she held him close.

He was her family now.

Author's Note

The Boy in the Suitcase is the first in a series of psychological mysteries entitled *The Concealing Sea*. More than a mystery, though, this is the story of a friendship that sustains two outsiders struggling against external threats and internal doubt.

A cruise ship provides an evocative venue for exploring classic themes of love, deception, fear and heroism. Some megaships boast passenger populations of more than five thousand, with another two thousand crew and service personnel as the semi-permanent population. Like many American small towns, cruise ships offer not only housing, but shops, restaurants, hair stylists, clinics, recreation, business services, sanitation and security. Unlike small towns, though, the people on board are largely strangers, and leaving town is not an easy option.

Many people provided assistance in the writing process. Sincere thanks to Michael Johnson of New Mexico State University for guiding me to gamma-hydroxybutyric acid and hyoscine hydrobromide, useful chemical compounds for the villains of this piece. I was delighted to work again with Joanna Pasek on the cover design. Early readers were instrumental in helping me polish the manuscript: Betty Bowie, Wendi Goen, Betty Harrison, Peter Goodman, Yosef Lapid and Susan Lapid. Others provided warm encouragement, including fellow Baltic Sea cruisers

Bob and Beth Czerniak. All inaccuracies and flaws, however, are entirely my own.

As always, my deepest gratitude goes to my best friend and cherished partner, on land and at sea, Peter Gregware.

About the Author

Photo by Sterling Trantham
sterlingtranthamphotography.com

N. V. Baker is a former political science professor and journalist. Before turning to fiction, she published three books of non-fiction, two in the field of presidential/legal studies.

Her debut novel **vanished.** drew in part on an overland journey she took from Bangkok to London from 1978 to 1979. **The Boy in the Suitcase** is her second work of fiction, and the first in the *Concealing Sea* mystery series. With her partner, Peter, she continues to travel. They live in the high desert in New Mexico.

Visit her on Facebook or at www.nvbaker.com

Also by N. V. Baker

vanished. A Novel.

An intrepid young traveler. A treacherous companion. An impossible journey home.

August 1978, and Cassie Robinette arrives in Afghanistan. Burning with curiosity about the world, she has traveled far, chronicling her journey west in long letters to her friend Jack Hunter. Near Kabul's Chicken Street, she meets two other foreigners and travels with them to Herat. A week later, they cross the border into Iran. The next day, Cassie vanishes...

Twenty-nine years later, Jack discovers her old letters, and they rekindle his love as well as a question that has always haunted him: why did Cassie stop writing?

Driven to solve the mystery, Jack is determined to find her. He mines her letters for clues and tracks down people she once knew. But in his worldwide quest for answers, he senses he isn't the only one on Cassie's trail. And if he isn't careful, his search could lead an old enemy straight to his long-lost love.

Critics call it:

"An excellent thriller with plenty of plot twists and turns, interesting characters, and unusual settings." (Manhattan Book Review)

"A great read." (San Francisco Book Review)

"A moving love story that isn't at all about the romance." (Readers' Favorite)